Death's Angel

After Dark
Book 5

Sarah Bailey

Please note the setting for this book is the United Kingdom.
The spelling throughout is British English.

Cover Art by Christian Bentulan

Published by Twisted Tree Publications
Visit their website at www.twistedtreepublications.com
Email them at info@twistedtreepublications.com

Paperback ISBN: 978-1-9996169-4-6

For the kindest soul I know - Sabrina
Your support is everlasting
Your friendship means the world
And my journey is enriched with you in my life

Contents

Chapter One

*A*lice wanted everything to stop for just one damn minute. How could she have been fooled by him for so long? *I'm such an idiot! Honestly, why did I ever believe he wanted a future with me?* She picked up a mug from the table, launching it at his head.

"I hate you. I hate you!"

Jason ducked, narrowly avoiding it. It crashed into the wall before shattering on impact with the floor. *I wish it had hit him. No less than he deserves.*

"Calm down."

He put his hands up.

"Don't you dare tell me to calm down! You're an arsehole. How could you? Three years. I've wasted three fucking years on you."

He didn't look remotely ashamed of his shitty behaviour. *I want to throw him out a window.*

"Come on, Alice, you know I care about you."

"Care about me? Don't make me laugh. If you cared so much about me, why have you been fucking other women behind my back?"

He flinched.

"They meant nothing to me."

"That's not an excuse. In fact, that's the worst excuse under the sun."

"Well, you're not exactly the easiest person to deal with."

Is he trying to make this my fault?

She stomped over to him, slapping his face, hard.

Shit, that's satisfying.

"Don't you dare try to turn this around on me. I didn't cheat on you."

He held his face, staring at her with shock.

"Alice..."

"No, Jason. I'm done. We're over."

She strode away. There was no way she was standing around arguing with him. He clearly had no remorse or shame. It was time she did what she should've done months ago.

"Where are you going?"

"Anywhere that's away from you."

She stormed into their bedroom, throwing clothes into an overnight bag. He followed her.

"Please, you can't just leave."

She ignored him, ripping her phone charger from the wall and tossing her makeup along with a hairbrush into the bag. She went into the en-suite, collecting her toiletries.

Just enough to get me through the next few days until I can work out what to do.

"Alice, don't do this."

She pushed past him back into the living room. She turned as she opened the front door to the flat.

"Fuck you, Jason. Don't try contact me again. We're done. Over. Finished. You can burn in fucking hell for all I care."

She slammed the door behind her, ignoring the pained expression on his face. He didn't get to make her feel bad for leaving. He was the one in the wrong. He'd cheated, not her. *How did I not see this coming?* He'd never been the best boyfriend, but she never imagined he'd go so far as to sleep with other people. She should've known. He'd been distant for months.

When she was outside the building, she faltered. Where was she going to go? She started walking. She would come up with something. She could stay in a hotel for the night. Strolling through Wandsworth Common, which was close to the flat, she sighed. The moon was high in the sky, but with all the light pollution, it was hard to see the stars. She'd only moved here to be with Jason and didn't know many people in London. Her best friend, Chris, moved to Edinburgh a few years ago and she rarely got a chance to see him. She supposed she should text him to let him know about her breakup, but she was too embarrassed. Chris never approved of Jason. He was going to say, 'I told you so'. She couldn't deal with that.

She spied a bench up ahead. Walking towards it, she sat down, placing her overnight bag next to her. She'd have to go home to get her stuff when she worked out what to do, but right now, she didn't want to see Jason. *I never want to see his stupid face again. I meant what I said. He can burn in hell.*

She looked to her right. There was a man sitting on the other side of the bench. She hadn't noticed him there before. His face was turned up to the sky. He had dark auburn hair, neatly styled, short at the sides and longer on top. His navy suit was immaculate.

He lowered his face and turned to her very slowly. He had bright green eyes. She knew she shouldn't be staring at him, but he was the most beautiful man she'd ever seen. She felt quite plain by comparison. She nudged her glasses up her face a little and blinked.

He has to be an angel. No normal man could look as stunning as him.

"You can see me?" he asked, startling her.

He was talking to her. To her. Plain Alice. She looked around, but the two of them were alone.

Why is he talking to me?

"Yes," she squeaked.

"That shouldn't be possible." His eyes narrowed. "What are you?"

What kind of question is that?

"Um... I'm just a girl. Why, what are you?"

He sneered. It marred his perfect face a little but didn't make him any less attractive.

"Don't you know?"

"No. Should I?"

"What is your name, girl?"

"Alice."

This was quite possibly the weirdest exchange she'd ever had with a stranger. *I'm not sure I should stick around to find out what this is about.*

"And what are you doing out here alone?"

"Um... Well, taking a walk I guess."

What was with this guy?

"What is with me is you're disturbing my peace and quiet."

She blinked. She hadn't said that out loud.

I know I didn't. Who is he?

"Honestly, you humans think far too loudly sometimes."

"What... how did you...?"

"You really don't know." He frowned. "Do you believe in Heaven?"

That was a weird question. Why would a stranger ask her about her personal beliefs?

"Well, I don't know. I mean it all seems a little bit far-fetched."

He shook his head, rolling his eyes.

"Well, if that's the case, you wouldn't believe me if I told you the truth."

"Try me."

She wanted to know what kind of ridiculous story he was going to concoct to explain why he'd heard what she'd thought.

"I am an Archangel. My name is Azrael."

This guy was certifiably crazy. *An Archangel?* She scoffed.

"Right.... That sounds entirely plausible."

"I knew you wouldn't believe me. Humans, tsk, all the same."

"If you're really an angel, why don't you have any wings?"

"I don't wish to bore you with all the reasons why it is a bad idea to have them on show."

She shook her head. Why was she even talking to him? She should be going to get a hotel room. Yet something stopped her. She wanted to know if he was telling the truth or not.

"Well, how do you expect me to believe you then?"

He sat there for a moment, pursing his lips. He stood up, straightening his jacket. He was very tall. He looked down at her with those dazzling green eyes. The intensity of his gaze pinned her to her seat. *Does he not have an off switch?*

"Humour me for one moment."

He cracked his neck, putting his arms out. Behind him, the air shimmered slightly before a huge pair of brilliant white wings unfurled from his back. It was quite possibly the most insane thing she'd ever seen.

"Holy shit," she breathed.

She blinked rapidly. She wasn't hallucinating, was she?

No. Those are most definitely wings.

4

"Yes, Alice. They are wings."

And he can hear my thoughts.

His lip quirked up at one side.

"Not all of them. Only the ones you're broadcasting too loudly."

"What is that supposed to mean?"

"It means I can hear you when you're thinking about me."

Then he must know what I was thinking when I first saw him.

"Yes, I'm well aware of your initial impressions."

She felt her face burning. Just because she thought he was drop-dead gorgeous, didn't mean she liked him. He seemed incredibly arrogant.

She couldn't deny what she was seeing. Azrael was an angel. She suddenly felt very small and insignificant.

Angels are real. What? How? I'm not crazy. He has wings and is the most stunning man I've ever seen. I don't have any other explanation.

"I think I believe you now."

He shook his head. A moment later, his wings disappeared. He sat down, staring at her face intently.

"Why do I detect a hint of sadness about you?"

She blinked, taken aback by his question.

"My boyfriend cheated on me."

The words came tumbling out against her will. She couldn't hold back. Something about Azrael made it impossible to say anything but the truth.

Could this night get any worse? I mean seriously, Jason cheats on me and then I can't keep my mouth shut around this... angel.

"And you decided to take a walk?"

"No, I stormed out of our flat and then realised I had nowhere to go."

He watched her for a moment before he stood again. He put his hand out to her. She looked at it, frowning.

"You are in need of a drink. Drowning your sorrows is something humans do, is it not?"

"Well, I should really be finding a hotel..."

"Do you really have the audacity to turn down an angel?"

"Turn down... You're not propositioning me, are you?"

He looked incredulous. His green eyes blazed for a moment.

"You mortals are so fixated on pleasures of the flesh. I am not attempting to lure you into bed by plying you with alcohol. Even if I wanted to do such a thing, I wouldn't need to engage in lowly mortal tactics, I assure you."

What did he mean he wouldn't have to engage in such tactics? Do women just fall at his feet? Well, if that's what he expects from me, he's got another thing coming.

Azrael raised his eyebrow. She flushed again. She wasn't sure why he wanted to have a drink with her, but she put her hand in his. He had the softest skin. Her fingers tingled. He tugged her to her feet.

"How am I meant to know why you'd want to take me for a drink?"

"I was merely being polite."

"Right."

Polite my arse. He wants something from me. I'm sure of it.

She knew he'd heard her, but she was glad he chose not to comment. He leant past her, picking up her bag and slinging it over one of his shoulders.

"I do thoroughly detest your human transportation contraptions."

Without warning, he tugged her into his arms before his wings unfurled again. She gasped, clutching him. They shot into the air. He held her close, soaring higher.

"Holy shit... won't... won't someone see us?" she called over the rushing sound of the wind.

"No. I am an angel. Disguising our presence is simple."

She wrapped her arms around his neck.

"Don't worry, I've got you."

He might have a hold of her, but it didn't make the experience any less terrifying. She looked past his shoulder. She could see the lights twinkling below them. London looked pretty from this height. He banked to the right, she clutched him tighter, closing her eyes. Was this actually her life right now? Only half an hour ago she'd been shouting at Jason and now she was flying over London in the arms of an Archangel, who apparently wanted to take her for a drink. *This is actually mental.* The wind rushed around her ears. She could only be glad of her short, brown hair. If it was any longer, it'd be flying in her face.

She felt them descending and opened her eyes again. The ground was rushing towards them at an alarming pace. She tried not to yelp, but he set them down lightly. She shook all over and wasn't quite sure she'd be able to stand up on her own. *How does he make that look so easy? My legs feel like jelly.*

"You can let go now," he said.

"I know," she whispered.

He stood patiently for a minute before he pried her arms off and set her on the ground. There was a sneer on his perfect face. She ignored it. He should've asked before he flew off with her.

"Come along."

He started walking up the dark street. She had to walk fast to keep up with him.

His legs are ridiculously long. In fact, he's ridiculously tall, ridiculously arrogant and ridiculously perfect.

She spied a slight upturn of his lips. She flushed. He could hear her when she thought about him. Cursing under her breath, she turned away. He stopped abruptly and she almost barrelled into him.

They were outside some steps leading down to a bar. The red neon sign read 'Fright Night'. She'd never heard of it before, but she didn't really know London very well. Two people were making their way up the steps. One of them looked up at them, their eyes widening. Azrael appeared markedly put out.

"I was hoping to avoid this," he muttered.

"You're... You're..." the man said, pointing at Azrael.

"Yes, yes, come here."

The man came up the stairs and stared up at him. The woman with him was frowning heavily.

"What are you doing, Frank?" she hissed.

"Can't you see? It's an angel," Frank replied.

"Who, that girl?"

"No. Him."

Frank pointed to Azrael again. The angel rolled his eyes, shaking his head.

"Mortals," he said to Alice before turning back to the man.

He leant down, whispering something in his ear before he kissed the top of the man's head. Alice had absolutely no idea what was going on. Azrael stepped back. The man stared up at him in wonder. She looked at the angel.

There was a seemingly ethereal light encasing him for a moment before it disappeared.

Holy shit, what was that?

"Thank you," he said.

"He won't be thanking me in a moment," Azrael said to her.

"Frank, I don't know what's gotten into you. I knew we shouldn't have come to this bar. It's full of weirdos," the woman said, tugging on Frank's arm.

"Oh, Julie, I wish you could see him. He's magnificent."

Azrael rolled his eyes again.

Does he have people swooning over him on a regular basis?

"No, just the ones who are about to meet their maker."

"What?" Alice asked, startled.

She watched the woman pulling Frank down the street. He seemed to be unable to drag his eyes away from the angel.

"Frank! Come along!"

"She's about to have a rude awakening," Azrael said.

Alice tugged on his sleeve. He hadn't answered her question. She didn't know why Frank could see him but not the woman he was with.

"What is going on?"

He frowned, brushing her hand away.

"Did I not explain to you who I am?"

"Yes, an Archangel."

"Does the name Azrael really mean nothing to you?"

"No... Should it?"

He stared at her for a full minute without speaking. She fidgeted under his intense gaze. Having the full attention of an angel was rather disconcerting.

Does he really have to stare at me like that? Does he have any idea how unnerving it is? No, actually probably not. He doesn't seem to care about anything other than himself.

"I am the Angel of Death. At least, that's what you mortals like to think of me as."

Chapter Two

*A*lice took a step back. *Angel of death? Does he kill people? Oh, why is this my life?*

"What... what's that supposed to mean?" she asked.

"It means I bring death to the world. Humans don't see me unless they're about to die. I can allow anyone to see me if I so wish it, but I don't care for the company of mortals."

The implications of what he'd just told her made her head hurt. This evening was too much for her to process all at once. How had she gone from having a breakup to being told Heaven and angels are real? She'd seen evidence of it in front of her.

Am I about to die?

"No, Alice, you're not going to die. We should discuss this inside."

He began to descend the steps into the bar. She hurried after him, not wanting to get stuck out there alone. The only person who could give her answers was the arrogant angel. She needed them desperately if only to stop the whirling thoughts in her head.

"But you just said people can't see you unless you let them. I'm going to look like I'm talking to myself."

She certainly didn't need people thinking she was nuts on top of everything else.

"Have a little faith."

He ignored the woman at the coat check, tugging open the door and striding into the bar. It was a modern looking place with a laid-back atmosphere. Azrael stood at the bar. She stepped up next to him, her head turned up towards his face. The confidence and poise which encompassed him was intimidating, but she couldn't let him ruffle her any further.

"Won't everyone know what you are?"

"No."

Does he ever give more than short answers? How am I supposed to understand any of this?

A woman with dark hair approached them.

"What can I get you?" she asked, looking directly at the angel.

"What would you suggest for someone whose boyfriend has just cheated on them?" he replied.

Alice's mouth dropped open. *What the hell? Did he really just say that? What is wrong with him?*

The woman raised an eyebrow.

"I know just the thing."

She turned away to set about mixing the drink. Alice wanted to hit him.

"You can't go around telling people that," she said.

"Why not?"

"Because it's private... and... and embarrassing."

Does he actually have any idea how to behave around humans? I don't know what his deal is.

He turned to her, his green eyes curious.

"You didn't seem to object to telling me."

She was silent. She hadn't wanted to tell him, but by some sort of compulsion, she felt the need to be honest. *And I wish I hadn't now.*

The woman set a drink in front of her. It was bright blue with a strawberry hooked over the top.

"And for you?" she asked.

"Nothing."

"That'll be seven eighty then."

He turned to Alice expectantly.

"What? You want me to pay for my own drink. You're the one who asked me here."

She dug around in her handbag, huffing. *Honestly, why did I even agree to this in the first place?* She dug out some money and handed it to the bartender.

"I have no need for what passes as currency in your world, usually," he said when the bartender returned, handing Alice her change.

She glared up at the angel. She was beginning to regret ever sitting down on that stupid park bench. He walked away over to an empty booth in the corner leaving her to follow behind. He set her overnight bag down and sat, folding one leg over the other. She slid into the booth next to him.

"Go on, ask your questions," he said, waving a hand at her.

"Why are we here?"

"They cater for supernatural types here. Fewer humans, less dealing with their idiocy."

"Wait, what?"

He shook his head, rolling his eyes.

"Did you not stop to think if angels exist then what other things might be lurking in the dark corners of the night?" He pointed to the bartender. "She's a vampire. Over in the corner, there are some werewolves and to your right, a fae or two."

She looked at each of the people he'd indicated. They looked normal to her until she realised the woman at the bar was grinning. She had fangs. Full on fangs. She turned away, taking a huge gulp of the blue liquid to calm her nerves. It burnt on the way down. She spluttered a little.

"Shit, that's strong."

She had no idea what was in it. She glanced back at the angel. He was watching her impassively.

"Explain this death thing to me. You said I wasn't about to die."

"You're not. There's nothing special about you, yet you can see me. I do not know what to make of you."

Nothing special? Of all the arrogant, irritating men... angels I could've run into.

"Is that why you decided I was worth giving your precious time to?"

"Yes."

At least he was honest. She was done with liars like Jason. It was pretty much the only thing the angel had going for him other than his looks.

"In fact, I've decided to keep you."

Her mouth dropped open.

Keep me? What is he on about now?

"Yes, until I work out why you can see me, I shan't let you out of my sight."

This was getting really ridiculous now. She wasn't going anywhere else with him.

"I don't remember signing up to be your human pet."

"I didn't say you had a choice."

She blinked.

Who does he think he is?

"You know who I am."

"Stop listening to my thoughts."

He chuckled, his green eyes lighting up for a moment.

"Stop thinking about me."

She folded her arms across her chest. *I should just leave.* Except where was she going to go? She didn't want to go back home to Jason. And she still had questions. She fiddled with the glass. Something about Azrael set her on edge.

"Why are you on Earth?"

"Because He commanded it."

He? Oh wait, he's talking about God.

"And what, you just have to obey?"

"It's beyond your mortal comprehension."

She took another sip of the blue drink, grimacing as it went down. The alcohol was beginning to dull her senses a little. She sat back, looking at him intently. His high cheekbones and pouty lips were more than she could take.

I wish he wasn't so stunning. It's distracting. A bit like looking up at a shooting star. The rare brilliance of it is a sight to behold.

His eyebrow raised. She knew he'd heard that, but she decided she didn't care. He clearly knew he was attractive.

"What else can you do then?"

It seemed like a pertinent question. She might never get another chance to speak to an angel.

"As an angel?"

"Well, yes. I mean, aren't you like all powerful beings?"

"We possess varying strengths and qualities. A scribe does not require the same level of abilities as an Archangel."

Why is he being so vague?

"That didn't answer my question."

"Explaining such things to mortals is tiresome."

If he wasn't going to explain things, then why did he even want her here? Nothing made sense any longer.

"Fine. What do you want to talk about then?"

"Nothing as such."

She wanted to squeal in frustration. She knocked back the rest of her drink, not caring that her throat was on fire. If he was going to be obnoxious, she wasn't sticking around. She was about to grab her bag so she could leave when his hand curled around her arm.

"Where do you think you're going?"

"Away from you for starters."

He pulled her towards him before cupping her cheek with his soft hand. He brushed her hair from her face.

"Sleep, Alice."

She didn't want to obey him, but her body went slack. She slumped in the booth. He held her head, staring down at her with those intense green eyes.

"I'm not letting you leave."

She closed her eyes as sleep tugged her under.

When Alice came to, she was lying in a strange bed. She turned her head. Azrael was standing with his back to her, one hand placed against a window frame, looking down at something below.

"Welcome back to the land of the living," he said.

She sat up. Her head felt funny. The sunlight was streaming in through the window, illuminating his auburn hair. Her breath caught in her throat. *Oh man! Why? Why can't I look away?*

"What did you do to me?"

"Sent you to sleep."

Her glasses were sitting on the bedside table. She pulled them on. She could see him more clearly. It was worse. Much worse. In the sunlight, he really looked like an angel. *A stunningly attractive angel who I apparently can't stop looking at. What is wrong with me?*

"So, what, because I wanted to leave, you thought it was acceptable to put me to sleep so I wouldn't escape?"

"Your presumption is correct."

She launched a pillow at his head, which he reached out and caught deftly.

"Are you always this grumpy in the morning?"

"Wouldn't you be if someone decided they wanted to hold you prisoner?"

"You're not a prisoner, Alice."

"Well, it feels like it."

She folded her arms across her chest.

"You said you had nowhere else to go, did you not?"

That's hardly the point. She shuffled off the bed. He'd taken her shoes off but left her in her clothes. Her bag was sitting on a chair in the corner. She went over to it, pulling out her hairbrush and makeup wipes. Her heart thundered.

I'm a frigging prisoner. How did I get in this situation?

She knew better than to object further. She wasn't dealing with just anyone. Azrael was an angel. She was pretty sure if she tried to run away, he'd just bring her back. There wasn't much she could do about it. There was a mirror nearby. She had severe bed hair. Tackling the chestnut coloured mess until it was in some semblance of order, she then removed her makeup. Staring at her grey eyes, she put her glasses back on. She wished she'd thought to bring her contacts.

She turned back to Azrael who hadn't moved from his spot by the window. There was something sad about him. She went over and stood next to him, staring down at the street far below them.

"Where exactly are we?" she asked.

"Close to the Barbican."

"Why would you want to live in the city?"

"I have no wish to be here at all. It is merely convenient."

"Are you not able to return home?"

"No."

His tone brokered no further questions.

He can't return to Heaven. How long has he been stuck here?

He didn't seem to be in the mood to comment on her thoughts. She shuffled away, picking up her purse and pulling her phone out. There was a message from Chris.

Call me when you're free!

She checked the time before she fired a message back. She was going to be late for work if she didn't get a move on.

Will do after work, love yah.

She looked up at Azrael again.

"I need to go to work."

"I told you, I'm not letting you out of my sight."

"I don't know what type of shit you lot do up in Heaven, but on Earth, this is kidnapping and following me around, stalking."

He turned to her. There was nothing in his expression which gave away his reaction.

"Fine, I'll take you to work. Happy?"

She wasn't, but she didn't voice that out loud. She turned away, digging through her bag. She was glad she'd packed a set of clothes for work, but she needed to go home and get the rest.

I don't want to see Jason, but I need my stuff. Still, I don't need Mr High and Mighty getting involved.

"If you want your things, you merely have to ask."

"Stop reading my mind and what do you mean I just have to ask?"

He strode over to her, taking her face in his hand. She froze, quite unable to move with him staring down at her. The attention of an angel, an Archangel, was disconcerting on so many levels. She could feel the power radiating from him. She felt something brushing, rustling through her mind.

"I'm more than just a perfect figure, Alice," he said.

He stepped back. Scattered all around the room were her things. Her mouth dropped open.

How is that even possible?

She looked up at the angel. He had a smug smile on his face.

"Um... wait... you, oh. Jason is going to wonder what the hell happened."

"I didn't think you cared about the cheater any longer."

She wished she didn't care anymore. Jason was a dick.

"It only happened yesterday. Feelings just don't go away on a whim."

"Mortals... Always with your emotions."

"So what, you'd rather us be robots?"

"At least you wouldn't cry all over me when you realise you're going to die. Humans are far too messy."

She threw her hands up. Talking to him was impossible. If he didn't like being near 'mortals', as he so lovingly called them, why did he want to keep her around?

"Well, that's too bad for you then, isn't it? You're the one who doesn't want to leave me alone. Boohoo, pity the poor angel stuck with the silly human girl."

He turned away, rolling his eyes.

Yeah, well, serves you right, mate.

"Where's the bathroom?"

"Over there."

He waved to a door behind her. She marched in. Her clothes fell out of her hands. It was huge. There were floor to ceiling windows looking out over London and a bath set in the middle of the room. A large shower situated on the left and a vanity with twin sinks on the right.

"Holy shit."

"I like open spaces."

She jumped at the sound of his voice. He'd followed her in.

"Um, I came in here to get changed."

"And?"

"Oh, just go away. Haven't you heard of the term privacy?"

"I'm not allowing you out of my sight."

"I'm literally in the next room. Where do you think I'll go? I'm not about to jump out of a window to escape you. I'm not stupid even if you think I am."

He looked as though he was about to argue with her further before he turned on his heel and left her to it. She stuck her fingers up at his retreating back. She didn't care what he said, she was essentially his prisoner. She hurriedly stripped out of her clothes and saw to her needs before he decided to change his mind about leaving her alone.

When she walked back out into the bedroom in a fresh set of clothes, it no longer looked like a bombsite with all her stuff scattered around. She walked over to the floor to ceiling sliding doors and checked inside. Her clothes were neatly folded and hung up on hangers next to his. Everything he owned was tailored to perfection.

Oh, this is his bedroom. Why would he put my stuff in here?

"It is mine, but I don't sleep often," he said.

"I don't remember agreeing to stay here with you."

"Agreement implies choice."

This wasn't getting her anywhere. It was clear he wasn't going to let her go any time soon. It wasn't as if she could think of anywhere else to stay. She couldn't go crawling back to her parents. It would be mortifying to admit what Jason had done. There was also the little factor of the angel who apparently wasn't going to let her out of his sight.

"You know what, you're impossible, but whatever. Let's just go. I'm going to be late as it is."

Chapter Three

Alice stomped back into the penthouse. He'd insisted on flying her to work and back because he hated the Underground. He was a nightmare, talking about how bored he was and trying to distract her every five minutes. She was surprised she'd gotten anything done. No one else was able to see him, but libraries were meant to be quiet places. Having him talking in her ear all the time was irritating. Throwing him off the roof of a building seemed like a wonderful idea.

"I don't know what you're so angry about," Azrael said, looking down at his nails.

"Oh, just go away. I want to be alone."

She slammed the bedroom door in his face, not giving a shit what he thought. Throwing herself down on the bed, she groaned. What had she gotten herself into? The damn angel had turned her life upside down in the space of twenty four hours. She did have to admit it was Jason who had started it by cheating on her. If she hadn't found out, she'd still be with that idiot and she'd never have met the beautiful angel who was still in his living room, probably confused by her behaviour.

Why do I even care anyway? He's the one who's holding me prisoner.

She shouldn't have any sort of feelings other than annoyance and disgust for Azrael, but somehow, she couldn't shake the feeling he needed someone to talk to. Could she be that person? She shook herself. That was the most idiotic notion she'd had all day.

It dawned on her she'd told Chris she'd ring him after work. She flipped over onto her back, grabbing her purse and tugging her phone out. He answered on the second ring.

"Ally, love, how are you?"

He was the only one she allowed to call her that. She'd never tell anyone else about his nickname for her. Especially not Azrael. *Damn it, that stupid angel needs to get out of my head. Like right now. I'm so fed up of him.*

"I'm all right. How's work?"

"You do not sound okay."

"Chris."

He always had a knack for knowing when something was up with her.

"Fine, fine. Work is good. I met a guy last weekend, but you know how it is, they always disappoint me in the morning."

She chuckled. Chris was forever picking the wrong men. He'd been the same when he'd lived in Kent. They'd met when they were kids, remaining the best of friends into adulthood.

"What was wrong with this one?"

"Oh, he expected breakfast. You know I don't cook. I offered to take him out, but by that time, I knew he wasn't the one for me."

"I think you're just a picky bastard."

He roared with laughter.

"Touché, darling."

"I really wish you'd stop going out to bars to meet them or going on Grindr, it really doesn't help your cause."

"Hmm... at least my sex life isn't as dull as a doorstop unlike yours."

Her laughter died in her throat.

"Um... about that..."

"Is this why you sound so down in the dumps?"

"Please don't say I told you so."

"What has the little worm done this time?"

She sighed. Chris had never liked Jason.

"He cheated on me."

She heard his sharp intake of breath.

"I told you that little fucker would break your heart. Alice, you should've kicked him to the curb a long time ago, love. Tell me, did you kick his butt?"

She snorted. As if she would resort to violence, but she kind of wished she had kicked him in the nuts. He would've deserved it.

"No, but I threw a mug at his head. Sadly it missed. Then I stormed out. I haven't been back. It's most definitely over."

She was never going back to Jason. There was no reason for her to go back to their flat. Not now Azrael had somehow brought all of her stuff here. *That damn angel. I suppose I should be grateful he's made sure I don't have to face Jason.*

"Where are you staying then? You don't know anyone in London."

How could she tell Chris about Azrael? He wouldn't believe her, would he? Would Azrael even be okay with her revealing his true nature to anyone? She didn't think he would.

"Uh... It's complicated."

She slapped her hand over her head. That was the worst thing she could've said.

"Ally, what have you gotten yourself into?"

"Nothing. I swear. I'm safe, Chris. I promise."

The door to the bedroom opened. Azrael was standing there with a frown on his face. It still almost hurt to look at his beauty.

Why the hell does he have to be so attractive and yet so damn irritating at the same time?

He cocked an eyebrow. She really needed to learn how to keep her thoughts under control.

"If you say so, but I wish you'd tell me. I'm worried now."

"Um, Chris, I have to go. I'll call you soon."

"Ally..."

"I'm sorry. I promise, we'll talk about it next time."

She hung up without letting him say anymore. Dropping the phone on the bed, she stared at the angel.

"Who was that?" he asked.

"My friend. I didn't tell him anything, I swear."

"I heard."

"Oh."

She should've known he could hear everything. At least she hadn't said anything he didn't already know. He advanced into the room, stopping by the end of the bed. His eyes raked over her. She felt distinctly uncomfortable.

"What do you want?" she asked.

"Aren't you hungry?"

On cue, her stomach rumbled. She flushed. That was slightly embarrassing.

"I guess so."

"There's food in the cupboards, make yourself something. You still need to take care of yourself."

And with that he turned and left. She stared after him. So much for him caring about her wellbeing. Her conversation with Chris rattled her a little. How was she going to ever explain Azrael to anyone? There wasn't a logical explanation for her staying with him. She didn't even know the real reason. Just because she could see him as an angel rather than whatever disguise he put on. It was a flimsy excuse. She wanted answers.

She got up, stomping into the living room. Azrael was sitting on the sofa, flicking through the TV channels. He looked up at her approach. She stopped right in front of him, glaring.

"I want you to tell me why you're keeping me prisoner."

"I already explained it to you," he said, staring at her impassively.

"No, you didn't. You gave me some bullshit about me being able to see you. That's not a reason."

"It's the only one you're getting."

She threw her hands up.

"You're fucking impossible, do you know that?"

He gave her a smile, which she wanted to wipe off his face.

"As if I care what a mere mortal thinks of me."

Of course he doesn't care. He doesn't care about anything other than himself. Arrogant prick.

"Then why are you keeping me here?"

"It's for your own safety."

She stomped her foot. She knew it was childish, but the angel in front of her did her head in.

"Why the hell would you care about my safety when you don't care about me?"

He rolled his eyes.

"It is my duty. Now, if you're quite done, I'm bored with this conversation."

She took a deep breath. He was sorely testing her patience.

You can just go to hell.

She strode away into the kitchen and ripped open the fridge. One day with the angel and she wanted to tear her hair out. Why did he have to be so damn attractive? It made her head hurt.

He had a surprising amount of fresh food. She didn't really care what she ate at that point. She was far too pissed off. Tugging out vegetables, she found he had noodles in the cupboard. A simple stir fry would do. Roughly chopping the vegetables, she threw them into a wok with sesame oil and followed it up with soy sauce. When the noodles were ready, she threw them in as well along with a few other ingredients. She'd made too much, but she didn't care.

Dumping it out onto a plate, she was about to turn around when she found she couldn't move. Azrael rested his hands on the counter either side of her. His body was far too close to hers. Her heart raced in her chest.

"You are not one of these women who rarely eats, are you?" he asked, his mouth next to her ear.

"N... No."

She'd always liked her food too much. Her mum had taught her to cook from a young age. She enjoyed making meals for her parents when she'd gotten older. Yet she couldn't understand why he was even asking that or why he'd caged her against the counter.

"Good."

"Can... Can you move?"

She turned in his arms, staring up into his dazzling green eyes. His lip quirked up at the side.

"Why? Do you not enjoy being close to me?"

"No. I don't."

Her body tingled all over. *That's a lie. He knows it. I know it.*

"Hmm, I think perhaps you're not quite telling the truth."

"Why on earth would I want to be near someone who drives me crazy every time they open their mouth?"

His smile grew wider. His arrogance clearly knew no bounds.

"Little mortal," he said, his voice quiet. "You are an enigma. A puzzle I wish to solve. One I am inexplicably curious about."

Alice's heart thumped wildly. His words were cryptic, but he was curious about her. Was it just because she could see him or was it something else entirely? *What else could he possibly want from me?* His eyes burnt with repressed emotions, searing into her soul. She felt his presence all around her. The hairs on the back of her neck stood on end, goose pimples ran down her arms. And something she never wanted or expected to feel started in her stomach and wound its way down to her core. Desire. The urge to throw herself at him, kiss him, tear his clothes off and have him inside her threatened to overcome all her common sense.

What the fuck is happening to me?

"Please, move," she whispered.

He stared down at her for the longest moment. His eyes still burnt as if he knew what she was thinking, exactly what he was causing inside of her. Then he stepped back and strode away. She took a breath she hadn't realised she was holding. Whatever he'd done to her, she wasn't sure she wanted a repeat of it.

I do not want him.

I don't.

I really don't.

Alice was thoroughly fed up with Azrael after a week. Neither of them had mentioned the strange interlude between them which set her whole world on fire. She sat at the breakfast bar in the kitchen swinging her legs whilst she ate the dinner she'd prepared for herself. The angel was lounging on the sofa, his arm resting on his face.

"I have no sympathy for you," she said. "You don't have to come with me to work."

"Tsk, mortals," he mumbled.

"You seem to be rather taken with this particular mortal right here."

"Do not mistake my keeping you here for interest in you."

"I didn't mean... Honestly, I got it the first time when you told me you weren't interested in, what was it you said... Oh yes, 'pleasures of the flesh'. For the record, I have no interest in you either."

"Hmm, then why do you wax poetic about my appearance in your head?"

She scowled and went back to her food. He really needed to quit this habit of listening to her thoughts. It was a complete invasion of privacy. So what if she thought he was beautiful? Didn't mean he had the personality to go with it.

Oh yes, I really want to get into bed with the angel keeping me prisoner, that's totally normal... not!

"Most mortals would relish the chance to fall into bed with an angel."

"They clearly haven't spent any time with you. It's only been a week and I already want to throw you off a building."

"That would only be an issue if I was human."

"Has anyone ever told you how annoying and arrogant you are?"

"On several occasions."

"What a surprise and you didn't stop to think you might be the problem?"

He didn't respond. She looked over her shoulder, but he hadn't moved. She slid off the stool and took her plate over to the sink. She washed up the dishes before moving into the living room. She sat down on the sofa across from him, pulling out her phone. She had several missed calls from Jason along with three voicemails she'd been avoiding listening to. It was time to face the music.

"Alice, please come home. I'm sorry. I won't do it again."

Delete.

"Did you come around and take all of your stuff whilst I was at work? That's so childish."

Delete.

"Alice, please, can we at least talk this through? Where are you staying? I miss you."

Delete. What an arsehole. As if I want to speak to him after what he's done.

"He sounds perfectly pathetic," Azrael said.

She glanced over at the angel. He'd moved his arm and was staring at her.

"As if it's any of your business."

"Wouldn't most mortal women be crying over such a thing?"

She'd cried when she'd found evidence of Jason's betrayal, but it'd quickly turned to anger.

"He's not worth crying over. Not anymore."

She felt a wave of sadness. By all accounts, she should be heartbroken, but he hadn't exactly been the best boyfriend. They'd drifted apart over the last year since she'd moved to London.

"Tell me, what did you see in this man?"

Having no idea why he'd want to know, she was in two minds about telling him.

"You'll just think I'm pathetic."

"I think most mortals are pathetic."

She turned away, unable to take his intense gaze any longer.

"Jason was charming, handsome, had a good job... All the things a woman should want in a man. I thought because he'd paid attention to me, it meant I was worthy of someone's affections. I'm beginning to think I was just an easy target because I was lonely."

She hated sounding so tragic. Loneliness was a killer. It made you do all sorts of stupid things.

Like staying with a man who didn't appreciate me.

She glanced at the angel. He was still staring at her, his expression unreadable.

"Do you get lonely?" she asked.

"Yes."

She hadn't expected him to answer so bluntly.

"Aren't there other angels on Earth?"

"If they weren't all so insufferable, perhaps I'd seek them out."

"Are you really telling me you have no one here you like to spend time with?"

"Lucifer is in Hell. I detest the place. My fellow Archangels wouldn't leave dear old dad's side. As if I'd want to see them anyway."

A wave of sadness threatened to overcome her.

"So... Lucifer is the only one you like?"

"Do you really not know the stories about me?"

She shook her head. He should've worked that out by now. She'd told him enough times she didn't know anything about him or his fellow angels.

"He threw us out of Heaven at the same time. Lucifer and I were close, once."

Her heart ached a little at the thought of him being alone for so long. Why she felt sorry for him was beyond her. *I don't even like him, so why do I feel like I understand his loneliness?* He was silent for a long time. He seemed so sad. It made her feel worse. She didn't like it. Having common ground with him wasn't what she needed. Especially after he'd made her feel all those weird urges only the week before.

"Azrael, I want to go for a walk."

She needed to clear her head. Her feelings about the angel in front of her were confused and conflicting.

"Fine."

He stood up abruptly. She had expected him to argue with her about it. She got up, collecting her coat before the two of them stepped into the lift. When they were outside, he looked at her expectantly.

"What?"

"Do you want to walk around the city or do you wish me to take you to a park?"

"A park, I guess."

He put his arms out, indicating she should step into them. She wasn't a fan of the whole flying business, but he refused to travel any other way. She wrapped her arms around his neck. Despite being in broad daylight in a public space, he shot into the sky with her.

"How come no one notices you taking off with me?" she asked.

"It's not just me I can hide from human sight."

He didn't say any more until he set them down.

"Is this acceptable?"

She looked around. They were in Hyde Park.

"Yes."

He dug his hands into his pockets and set off, leaving her following a little way behind him. He really was dead set on this whole keeping her in his sight business. Just because she could see him even when he hid himself from humans, didn't mean she needed constant observation.

It was a nice evening, dusk was setting in. She was glad she'd brought her coat. The air was crisp. It wasn't like being home in Kent where she'd grown up, but it was nicer than the polluted streets full of traffic.

Azrael stopped abruptly, causing her to walk into his back. She rubbed her head, adjusting her glasses. Before she had a chance to ask him what he was doing, a pair of hands pulled her backwards. She yelped.

The angel turned, his eyes narrowed.

"Now, come along quietly, little lady," said a gruff voice in her ear.

Chapter Four

Alice froze. Whoever this was, she had no interest in being kidnapped. Not after Azrael had already done so the night they'd met.

"Excuse me? Let go!"

When she looked back, there was a man with horns and red eyes dragging her away. Had he not noticed an angel standing in front of them?

Wait, why does he have horns? Is... is he a demon?

"I suggest you release her."

The demon looked up before he stopped. She turned to Azrael. He glowed softly, his magnificent wings protruding from his back. *Damn. It almost hurts to look at him. Why? Why does he have to look so... so... incredible?*

"What the fuck?" the demon exclaimed.

Clearly, he hadn't been expecting Azrael to be with her.

"I said unhand her, hell spawn."

"She's coming with me, angel."

The demon wrapped a hand around her throat, squeezing a little. She clawed at it. He was hot, unbearably so. *What does a demon want with me? This makes no sense. Has Azrael been keeping this from me?*

"You have no business with her."

"Don't I? You know nothing."

Azrael took a step towards them. She trembled. She was stuck between an angry Archangel and a demon. This was not how she wanted to spend her Friday night, but her life wasn't exactly normal anymore. Not since she'd encountered the angel in front of her.

"Give her to me."

"He wants her "

Azrael's green eyes blazed.

"I don't care what he wants."

The next moment the demon was shoved ten feet back and Azrael was by her side. It all happened so fast she barely registered it. He looked down at her for a moment, green eyes softening. It made her heart flutter restlessly in her chest.

"Do you see why I am keeping you in my sights?" he asked.

She nodded, still shaking. She didn't know whether to be terrified or relieved. *He saved me. He actually saved me. And the way he's looking at me like he cares about me... I don't understand.*

The demon got up, brushing himself off. The angel glared at him.

"You shouldn't stand in his way," he said.

"Tell him if he wants her, he can come to Earth and ask me for her himself," Azrael replied.

The demon glared before slinking away into the treeline. Azrael turned back to her.

"Can we go, please?" she whispered.

She no longer felt safe out in the open. The sanctity of Azrael's penthouse was far more appealing. He didn't say anything when he took her in his arms. She clutched his neck, burying her face in his shoulder. She didn't know who they'd been talking about nor why anyone would want her. Wrapped up in his arms, soaring across London, she couldn't help but feel as though there was a lot Azrael wasn't telling her.

She was still trembling when they reached the penthouse. He'd been silent and broody the whole way back. When she didn't move from the hallway, he looked over his shoulder at her.

"What's wrong?"

She couldn't answer. She hadn't really thought much about what else existed beyond Azrael. He'd pointed out vampires and werewolves, but the possibility of demons hadn't entered her mind even when he'd spoken about Lucifer. It was all very overwhelming.

He walked back towards her, his green eyes narrowing. He let out a long-suffering sigh before he took her coat off her and hung it up in the cupboard next to them. The next moment, he pulled her into his chest and held her, running a hand down her back in a soothing motion.

"Honestly, humans," he muttered.

He's so warm and comforting.

She wasn't exactly best pleased to feel that way about being held by Azrael. Her heart slammed against her ribcage, pounding in her ears. Her glasses were squished up on her face. She turned it to the side, laying it on his chest. He felt like any other human, except he exuded power. His own heartbeat thudded against her hand.

After a few long minutes, her limbs relaxed, trembling subsiding.

Thank you.

She didn't wish to voice it out loud, but she'd thought it at him.

"You're welcome."

She didn't want him to let go, but she imagined this was making him uncomfortable. He'd told her enough times he didn't enjoy the company of mortals like her. She stepped away. His arms dropped. She dared look up at his face. There was a hint of sadness in his expression.

"What aren't you telling me?"

"About why a demon tried to take you to Hell?"

"Well, yes, that and who you were talking about with him."

"He was referring to my brother."

"Lucifer?"

"One and the same."

"Why does he want me?"

This was becoming increasingly complicated. First, she'd been taken by Azrael against her will and now, the Devil wanted her.

What is with these angels?

"Do you think I know the inner workings of his mind?"

"No. I just don't understand any of this."

She turned away, walking into the living room, feeling exhausted. The last few days had taken it out of her. Being around an Archangel was draining. Constantly looking at someone so beautiful and breathtaking was just about enough to send anyone crazy. The ethereal glow emanating from him was almost too much to bear. It didn't stop her wanting to look at him. Wanting to be close to him.

Damn it. I don't want to feel this way.

"Feel what way?"

She jumped.

I hate it when you do that.

"What is it you feel, Alice?"

"Nothing. I don't feel anything."

It was a lie. She didn't like feeling anything for the angel. She hated how attractive he was. She didn't want to feel sorry for him nor did she want to admit to finding his warm, solid body more than a little distracting. And that night he'd pressed her up against the kitchen counter still plagued her senses.

"I'm going to bed."

She walked away to the bedroom, not caring if he'd been listening to her thoughts. Not caring if he came with her and insisted on her telling him how she felt. It was far too early to sleep, but she couldn't deal with sitting around with him all evening. She wanted him to stop treating her like she was some sort of inconvenience to him, but that wasn't going to happen anytime soon.

She shrugged off her cardigan and unbuttoned her blouse. She turned towards the door as she undid the last button. He was watching her, green eyes dispassionate.

Are you going to just stand there and stare at me?

He didn't answer her. She hesitated. Was she really going to undress further in front of him? She didn't know what he was thinking nor why he was even there. His eyes roamed down her chest. His gaze wasn't quite predatory, but it wasn't exactly innocent either.

Fine. If you're going to look, look.

She tugged it off, allowing it to flutter to the ground. The angel didn't move. Tension rippled between the two of them. She wondered who was going to snap first. Being almost topless in front of him made her face heat up. She didn't think she was unattractive, but he was an angel and he'd said he wasn't interested in humans. Judging by the fact that he couldn't stop looking at her, she wasn't quite sure if he'd been telling the truth. There was a hint, a flicker of emotion behind his eyes.

What are you going to do, Azrael? Stand there, leave or...?

She couldn't bring herself to finish the sentence in her head. She knew he'd heard her. His lip twitched, gaze intensifying a hundred fold. She wasn't prepared for the way he looked at her. It was almost as if his eyes were burning into her skin, leaving her flesh hot to the touch.

He looked away, breaking the spell. She took a long, steadying breath. He strode back into the living room leaving her feeling like she'd just won a very important battle between the two of them.

The victory was bittersweet and left her with a sour taste in her mouth.

Pacing the room like a caged animal, Azrael cursed. Just what he needed, a strange fascination with a human woman. Keeping her here was a terrible idea, but now he knew Lucifer wanted Alice, he couldn't allow her to leave. Was it starting? Was this the end?

He wished their father hadn't been so cryptic before he'd thrown them out. The words rang in his ears.

"You will only bring death to this world, my son. The Darkness is coming. It is coming for all of you. Azrael, you will bring the end."

What did He mean by me bringing the end?

Images of Alice's skin flashed through his mind. He slammed his hand on the window, careful not to break it. It was the last thing he needed.

Is this His idea of a joke? Does He think I want to want a human? I'm not some common mortal, lusting after her body. And yet... her skin, the curve of her waist...

He tugged at his hair, trying to tamp down the frustration he felt. He'd never wanted anything from mortals, but he wanted something from her. And so did his brother. He couldn't understand it. If Lucifer had only told him what their father had said to him. Would it make any of this clearer?

He walked back into the bedroom, unable to stay away from her any longer. She was tucked up in bed. His bed. Her glasses sat on the bedside table, her fingers curled around the blankets. He sat down next to her, stroking her hair from her face. She didn't stir.

Why do I feel this way, Alice? Why do I feel anything for you? And why won't you admit you feel it too?

He knew of her admiration of his physical appearance. It made him smile when he heard her thoughts. She couldn't hold them back.

Feeling emotions wasn't something he had much experience with despite living on Earth all this time. He'd been with human women to pass the time, but the physical pleasures were for their benefit rather than his.

This is foolish. A foolish human endeavour. And yet, he wanted to hold her again. She was so fragile. So human. He'd felt a spark of something in his chest when he'd given her comfort earlier. Then seeing her without a shirt made that spark turn into a flame. One which threatened to consume him whole.

He clicked his fingers. His clothes changed from a casual shirt and trousers to a soft t-shirt and bottoms. He pulled back the covers and slipped in next to her. He hesitated for a moment before curling himself around her back, wrapping an arm around her small waist. She stirred a little then, leaning into him.

"Az..." she murmured.

He froze. *Az? Is she dreaming about... me?* He knew the cheater was called Jason, so it couldn't possibly be him. Having her so close gave him an uncomfortable stirring in his stomach. He shouldn't be doing this, holding her whilst she slept. He buried his face in her neck, breathing her in. *I need to let her go.* He turned her face towards him, staring down at her mouth.

What would it feel like to kiss her?

She stirred, eyes cracking open before she blinked.

"What... What are you doing?"

"Why the hell is he in bed with me? Holding me? Why... Why does it feel so nice?"

He wasn't quite sure how to explain his presence. He didn't know why he was here himself. She wasn't moving away. She was staring at him with those warm, grey eyes of hers. The ones he felt like he could drown in.

"Azrael?" she whispered.

"Go back to sleep, Alice."

"But you're..."

"His face is so close. Why won't my heart stop thumping? Why does he make me feel all hot? I'm not... I'm not really attracted to him, am I? I thought I was, but this...

No. No. Oh, holy shit. No, this can't be happening. I can't feel this way about him. He's annoying, cryptic and doesn't even like humans."

He tried not to smile. She knew he could hear everything. Her face was bright red. She wanted him. They both knew it. What Alice didn't know is he wanted her too, although for the life of him, he couldn't understand why.

"Stop listening," she whispered.

"And not get to hear how you really feel?"

She glared at him, stiffening in his grasp.

"Azrael, I have no idea why you'd think it's okay to get in bed with me whilst I'm asleep nor start touching me. Neither of those things are normal or acceptable behaviour."

His eyes were drawn to that mouth she was using to tell him off. The mouth he wanted to explore.

"This is my bed."

"You said you don't sleep."

"Doesn't mean I can't."

She turned to him fully.

"Fine. If you're going to insist on being in here, I'm going to lay down some rules. Firstly, you're not allowed to cuddle me and secondly, you need to stay over there."

She pointed to the other side of the bed.

"Is that so?"

"Yes."

"I object to both of those rules."

"I don't care."

"He's so irritating! I wish my heart would calm down. It's making this impossible. Why won't he stop staring at my mouth? First, he wants to watch me undressing, now cuddling me in my sleep? I don't get him."

He was staring at her mouth because he had the undeniable urge to kiss her. He cupped her cheek, running a thumb over her bottom lip. She looked at him, shock in her expression. She was moments away from giving into what was between them. He could feel it.

"Az... please, stop," she whispered.

She was dreaming about me.

He released her. The plea in her voice was too much. He shifted back, giving her the space she wanted. She shuffled away, putting further distance between them. She turned, facing away from him. He lay on his back, staring up at the ceiling.

"What the fuck is wrong with me? I didn't really want him to stop holding me. I'm insane. Why did he look like he was going to kiss me? And why did I want him to?"

A small mewl of frustration left her lips. Her thoughts and what came out of her mouth painted two very different pictures of Alice's feelings towards him. He knew better than to press her. It might well push her away further. He wanted to see her smile, not be angry at him.

Why do I have the ridiculous urge to want to make her happy?

Chapter Five

*A*lice awoke to find him still there. He was lying on top of the blankets, staring up at the ceiling. Her face burnt. He'd cuddled her last night. She couldn't quite believe it when she woke up to find him wrapped around her back. It'd made her feel things for him yet again that she wasn't comfortable with.

I wanted him to hold me closer. I wanted him to kiss me. I desire him. I'm clearly certifiable.

"Good morning," he said.

"Um, morning."

Oh, fuck. He just had to be listening to me.

She might as well get straight to the point. There shouldn't be any misunderstanding between them.

"You know, last night, that can't happen again."

"Fine."

That's it?

"Yes, Alice, that's it. You made it very clear how you feel."

She turned to him, frowning. She didn't expect him to just accept it like that. Besides, he'd heard her thoughts. He knew she wanted him. Knew she was lying. Why wasn't he making a bigger deal out of this?

Why do I feel so disappointed?

She shook herself. Shuffling out of bed, she wanted to be away from him. She needed to compose herself. She went into the bathroom, locking the door to keep him out. Not that a locked door could keep an angel out if he really wanted to get in.

She stripped out of her clothes and stepped into the shower. The warm water cascaded down her back. He made her feel so flustered when he was close. She couldn't deny she liked having him hold her. She liked it far too much.

I shouldn't feel this way about him. He's an immortal being from Heaven. It's completely inappropriate for me to lust after him.

She placed her hands on the glass to steady herself. Thoughts of what it'd be like to have his skin against hers, his fingers in places they shouldn't be assaulted her senses. Mentally chastising herself, she washed her hair and got out. She snagged a towel from the rack and dried her hair so it was no longer dripping. She wrapped another around her, drying off the excess water.

She walked out into the bedroom and stopped dead. Azrael's eyes were on her, pinning her in place. They roamed down the length of her body. Her face burnt. She hadn't expected him to still be in here. She coughed, but he didn't look away. The intensity of his gaze made her heart flutter. Her feet started to carry themselves towards him of their own accord. She stopped a foot away, staring up at him.

"What are you doing?" she asked.

"Looking at you."

"I can see that, but why?"

"Do I need a reason?"

His eyes grazed over the skin showing above her towel. She hiked it up, making sure she wasn't exposing herself any further.

"No, but I want to get dressed."

"By all means."

She pointed to the door. His mouth curved up at one side.

"You didn't seem to mind giving me a show last night."

Her face burnt hotter. There was nothing she could say to that. *Why is he acting like this now when he said he understood my terms about the bed? I'm so confused.*

"Just... get out."

He took a step towards her, closing the distance between them.

"Are you sure?"

She wasn't sure of anything, but she didn't appreciate him teasing her when it was blatantly obvious he wasn't serious. He'd told her from the beginning he wasn't interested in humans. Wasn't interested in her.

"I'm sure as hell not about to drop my towel in front of you if that's what you're implying."

"There's something about you, Alice. I'm going to find out why you can see me, one way or another."

And with that, he turned on his heel and strode out leaving her staring after him.

What the actual fuck was that about?

She took two steps back and slumped on the bed. The angel was far too confusing for words. One moment he was acting like she was an inconvenience to him. The next, teasing her, touching her, making her feel like fire ran in her veins. She let out a little mewl of frustration.

Fine. If he's going to be all weird and confusing then whatever. I don't have the energy to work out what the hell he really wants with me.

It was enough she was practically his prisoner. Although she had to admit, she didn't want a recurrence of a demon trying to make off with her. Staying with Azrael was her best option. There wasn't anyone safer than an Archangel, right?

She padded out into the open plan living space when she'd dressed. It was the weekend so she wouldn't have to deal with him complaining all day. Yesterday had been an absolute nightmare. She sighed.

Azrael was sat at the breakfast bar, twirling a fork. She walked over, perching on the stool next to him.

"What's this?" she asked.

Two mugs of tea sat with two plates piled high with pancakes, fruit and maple syrup.

"Breakfast."

"Since when do you need to eat?"

"I don't."

"Doesn't mean you can't. Right. I get it."

She picked up the knife and fork and dug in. She almost groaned. It tasted incredible. Glancing over at the angel, she found him watching her with an inscrutable expression.

"Um, thank you. It's really good," she said after she'd swallowed her mouthful.

He didn't respond, merely turning to his own plate. She hadn't seen him eat or drink before.

"Do you actually like human food?"

"Not all of it is terrible." He tucked into his pancakes, chewing and swallowing. "Everything tastes better with an angel's touch."

She rolled her eyes and went back to her own meal. They ate in silence for a while. She hugged the mug of tea to her chest, wondering what he was thinking.

"Would you like to do something today?" he asked, startling her.

"Like what?"

Does he actually want to hang out with me? That can't be right.

"What do you usually do at the weekends?"

"When I lived with my parents, I used to help them on the farm, but since I moved to London... Jason isn't one for fresh air, so it was usually the pub."

"You lived on a farm?"

"Yes, a dairy farm, but I tended to help my mum with her side business, selling homegrown vegetables at the farmer's market."

He eyed her for a moment. She popped the mug back down on the breakfast bar.

"You like the outdoors. In that case, why don't I take you home?"

"What?"

"To see your parents."

"Take me home to Kent... Why would you do that?"

"Wouldn't it make you happy?"

She had no idea how to react.

Since when does he care about my happiness? Also, how does he expect me to explain him to my parents? They don't even know I broke up with Jason.

"I appreciate the offer, but I'm not sure that's a good idea."

He leant towards her, his eyes fixated on her mouth. She jerked back in surprise, toppling off the stool. His arm shot out, curling around her back to stop her descent. He pulled her towards him, his body flush with hers.

"Careful," he said, his voice so low it sent a tingle up her spine.

Her entire body was on fire. Heat sizzled between the two of them. She couldn't look away from his dazzling green eyes.

"There's something lurking behind your eyes," he whispered. "Something which makes you so much more than just a girl. Perhaps it's why my brother wants you. Perhaps it's why you can see me."

"I don't know what you're talking about."

"No... you wouldn't. It's hidden, itching to get out."

She couldn't breathe. He was staring at her so intently. Her face burnt. It was all she could do to keep from trembling. From revealing exactly how much he affected her. He pulled away, settling her back on the stool. She gripped the counter to keep herself upright. He waved a hand, the plates disappearing before he walked away, leaving her wondering what on earth had just happened between them.

A little later, she escaped into the bathroom whilst he was still in the living room. She couldn't take it any longer. He was too confusing. She pulled out her phone. There was nothing for it. She needed advice.

"Ally, darling, to what do I owe this pleasure?" Chris said when he answered.

"I need your help."

"Does this happen to have anything to do with what you wouldn't tell me before?"

"Yes. I need you to listen to me carefully. This is going to sound insane. All of it. I barely even know where to start."

"Darling, start at the beginning. Whatever it is, I'll listen."

The words came rushing out. From her meeting Azrael, him keeping her here in his penthouse, who he really was, the fact that demons and Lucifer were after her. All of it. She held nothing back. Chris didn't interject once.

"I don't understand him. He seems like he wants something from me, but then he pulls away. I don't even know if I like him really. I mean he's an angel. Isn't it completely wrong and insane for me to feel anything? I just don't know. It's all such a mess."

Dumping all of that on Chris wasn't entirely fair, but she had no one else to talk to. She certainly wasn't going to broach the subject with Azrael himself.

"Well, fuck. Darling, Ally, tell me everything you've just said is the complete truth?"

"Do you think I'd make something that fucking crazy up?"

"No, but you're really telling me all that supernatural bullshit we hear about is true?"

"Yes."

"Fuck."

"Fuck indeed."

They were both silent for a long moment. Alice sat on the edge of the bath. She was confused and felt utterly alone. She wished Chris was here with her. He'd know what to do. He always did.

"This angel, Azrael... It sounds to me like he does like you on some level. I very much doubt he's admitted it to himself."

Of course he doesn't like me. What could he like? I'm just a plain girl who apparently can see angels.

"That makes no sense. He hates humans."

"Alice, darling, that man has been flirting with you. Did you not say he all but outright asked you to get naked in front of him?"

"That wasn't flirting. He was being a dick and trying to get a rise out of me."

Chris was talking nonsense. Azrael wasn't interested in humans. She was sure he just enjoyed winding her up. It was some kind of game to him.

"You have always been oblivious to others' feelings towards you."

"Seriously, he is adamant about not liking humans. Why would he like me anyway? All I've done is been an inconvenience to him. At least that's how he acts."

It wasn't strictly true. He'd offered to take her to her parents.

"Whatever you say, darling."

The bathroom door slammed back. She turned, staring at the angel. Azrael's eyes were blazing.

"Um... shit. Chris, I have to go."

She hung up without saying any more, placing her phone on the edge of the bath and standing up. Azrael was pissed. She was in for a difficult conversation. Why had she forgotten he was able to hear her conversations? *I'm a fucking idiot.*

"You told another human about this?" he said, fury in his voice.

"What else did you expect? You won't explain anything to me."

He strode over, taking her by the arm and pulling her towards him. He stared down at her, his expression still thunderous.

"You were meant to keep your mouth shut. You are aware my brother is after you. Did you not think about the risks you're taking involving someone else?"

Her heart dropped. Had she put Chris in danger by telling him? She'd made this into an even bigger mess than it was before.

"I'm sorry," she whispered. "I needed someone to talk to. He's my only friend."

The fire in his eyes dimmed a little.

"Talk to me."

"How can I? You're so unapproachable. You've told me more than enough times you don't care about me. You don't care about humans. I'm just your duty. A duty you seem to despise."

He flinched at her words, letting go of her abruptly. His eyes flashed with pain and bewilderment.

"You're not..."

"Not what?"

"A duty."

"Then what?"

Something else dawned on her. If Azrael knew she'd been talking about him to Chris, then he'd known what Chris had said about him flirting with her. She wanted to bury her head in her hands. *This is the single most embarrassing moment of my life. Chris is wrong. He's never flirted with me.*

"I want to know why you can see me and why... Why we... Why I..."

She'd never seen him flustered before. He ran a hand through his hair.

"Just know that you're not some kind of duty to me. I told you I would keep you safe and I intend to do that, but it's not because it's my duty."

He turned away, striding from the room before she could ask him any further questions. *What the actual fuck? One minute he's mad at me, the next he's stuttering over his words?* Alice shook her head. Whatever was going on between her and Az was a mystery.

Az.

She supposed that was how she thought of him now. She wasn't sure when it had happened, but somehow, she felt things for the angel that she shouldn't. And she was very sure he couldn't feel the same way about her, could he?

Chapter Six

Alice was done with his brooding. Azrael was an enigma. After that strange interlude between them where he'd revealed there was something inside her and the argument later over her telling Chris about him, he'd kept his distance for two very long weeks. It bothered her far more than it should.

Her cheeks grew hot every time she thought about his body pressed up against her. Being so close to him stirred her senses. She ached with longing when she looked at him.

Is that why he's staying away from me?

She surreptitiously watched him whilst they had the TV on. He wasn't paying attention, merely lounging on the other sofa. She fiddled with her phone. Jason had been calling her on and off, but she never answered. He hadn't gotten the message.

She'd been texting Chris. It was safer than calling him considering Azrael could hear their every word. Neither of them could make head nor tails of the angel's behaviour. Everything about him was confusing. From the fact that he'd told her he hated humans to when he'd said he didn't see her as his duty. *Then what does he see me as? I wish he hadn't just walked away that day.* He'd refused to speak to her on the subject. She gave up trying to broach it.

She looked at Azrael again. His auburn hair was ruffled from where he'd run his hand through it. He was so effortlessly sexy. It made her head hurt. Every part of her burnt whenever their eyes met. She hated admitting that she was no longer indifferent to him.

I can't understand why I want him. I don't even like him, do I? That's the problem. I think I do. I think I like him more than I really ever wanted or expected to.

His eyes met hers, one brow raised. She hastily looked away, knowing he was questioning what she was thinking. She couldn't stay in the same room as him any longer. She got up, intending to go have a bath just for something to do.

She got three steps from the bedroom when she felt his hand on her arm. She turned around, staring up at him.

"Where are you going?" he asked.

"Away from you."

"Why?"

"You know why."

"I don't think I do."

"Why would I want to be around someone who won't even speak to me? I've never felt so alone. Even when I was with Jason, I never felt like I was an inconvenience to him, but here, with you, that's all I feel. I'm tired of it."

There was confusion in his expression. The whole thing was exhausting.

He just doesn't get it. I don't even know why I'm trying to explain. He's never going to understand how I feel.

Looking at him made her heart thump. He no longer hid his angelic nature from her or maybe it was just because he couldn't. There was always a soft glow around him. It hurt to look at him, but that's all she wanted to do. She couldn't help it.

Azrael tugged her towards him, his hand on her face, tipping it up. She was so startled by his sudden movement, she didn't even protest.

"You're right. I don't understand, but I know what you want from me. I can't ignore what's between us any longer."

His eyes were on her mouth. He leant down, not giving her time to object before he kissed her. All the blood rushed to her head. His lips were incredibly soft. He pressed her closer. Kissing him was almost euphoric. Her skin tingled where he was touching it. Her hands were slack at her sides, his closeness, his lips, assaulting all her senses.

What... what is he doing? I didn't ask for this. I never asked him to kiss me no matter how many times I wished he would. This isn't fair.

She brought her hands up, shoving him away from her. Despite feeling bereft when his mouth was no longer on hers, she stared up at him with anger. The resounding slap across his face rang in both their ears.

"Don't you touch me! Don't you... just don't!"

Her chest heaved. She was angry at him for presuming and angry at herself for enjoying it, for wanting him to kiss her senseless. He hadn't flinched when she'd slapped him, his expression impassive.

"You dare try that shit again, I swear I'm going to leave. I don't care if you come after me. I'm not your human toy. Don't play games with me."

She strode away into the bedroom. She stood in the middle of the room, panting and ran a hand through her hair. Her heart hammered, her skin thrumming from where his hands had been on her.

An Archangel just kissed me. Me. Does he like me?

Nothing about it made any sense. He hadn't shown any interest in her other than wanting to know why she could see him. Why did he want to kiss her now?

She turned, feeling his presence. He filled the doorway, his green eyes roaming over her. He strode towards her. She sucked in a breath, backing away until she was against the window. He slammed a hand down above her.

"What have I done to make you think you're a toy to me, Alice?"

She gulped, quivering at the intensity of his presence. He wasn't holding back. Not one bit.

"What else do you call kissing me when you don't even like me?"

He leant down until his mouth was next to her ear.

"I've never told you I don't like you. It is quite the opposite."

She trembled.

Wait, what? What does he mean it's the opposite? Does... does that mean he wants me in the same way I want him? That's impossible.

"What do you mean?"

"Were you not listening when I said you are not my duty? No, Alice, you are more than that. So much more. Being near you drives me crazy."

His breath on her ear made her heart pound faster. She wanted him to kiss her again. It was insane, but it was the truth. His tongue curled around the back of her ear. It made her twitch.

"What are you doing?" she whispered.

"Daring to try again."

His lips peppered her jaw before they met hers. His kiss was more forceful this time. He took one of her hands, holding it above her head, pressing against her. Blood pounded in her ears. His solid body was warm and inviting. Her free hand curled around his back as she responded to his advances. She couldn't help it. Kissing him was the single most incredible experience of her life.

Is this what being on drugs feels like? Shit, he's just... so... powerful.

His other hand cupped her face, deepening the kiss. His tongue against hers felt like fire. She emitted a small moan of pleasure.

Don't stop, please, don't stop, Az.

Begging him to continue in her head was mortifying, but he didn't let up. Everything was centred on where his skin met hers. She couldn't think straight.

Kissing an angel was nothing like kissing a human. The two were incomparable. Heat pooled inside her. She wanted to touch him, to feel all of him. She ached with desire, longing. She wanted him. Wanted his hands all over her body. His skin against hers.

Why the hell do I want this? Why can't I stop thinking about what it'd be like to be naked with him?

She felt him smile against her mouth for a moment.

Oh, crap. I need to learn how to control my thoughts around you.

"Do you want me to take you to bed, Alice?" he whispered, pulling away.

She couldn't speak. He was staring at her with heat, passion, fire.

Did she?

She wanted his mouth on hers again. She didn't want to think about the implications, the consequences of what they were doing.

Kiss me, please. I want what you're offering me.

He let go of her hand, cupping her face with both of his. He pulled her away from the window. Throwing caution to the wind, they kissed each other again. He walked her over to the bed, pausing for a moment to pluck the glasses from her face. He placed them carefully on the bedside table. He pressed her down on the bed, covering her body with his own.

"Wait," she said.

He paused, looking down at her. The soft glow he emitted made her heart stop. He was so ethereally beautiful it made her head hurt. She didn't really want him to stop, but she had to ask him something before they continued.

"Do... do you actually want to do this?"

"Kiss you?"

"Well, yes, that and..."

The unspoken question hung between the two of them. Did he want to sleep with her or was he going through the motions because it's what he thought she wanted?

He opened his mouth to reply, but he froze the next moment.

"Lucifer," he growled.

"What?"

"He's here."

He rolled off her abruptly, getting off the bed the next moment. Her heart wrenched painfully at the loss of his presence.

Stop it, heart!

"Here?"

"On Earth. I need to go." He looked down at her. "Stay here, Alice. Don't leave under any circumstances. Do you understand?"

She nodded. It couldn't be good news if the Devil himself had risen. He began to move towards the door. She tore off the bed.

"Az!"

He paused in the doorway. She ran to him, wrapping her arms around his back. She pressed her face into the solid wall of muscle.

"Don't get hurt," she whispered.

She didn't know why she was worried about him. He was one of the most powerful beings in this world.

"I won't."

His voice sounded cautious. He turned in her arms, his dazzling green eyes meeting hers. Whatever he saw in her expression, made his soften. He cupped her face.

"I'll return to you. I fully intend to finish what we started."

He pressed a kiss to her forehead, but it wasn't enough. She caught his face before he could pull away. She pressed her mouth to his. Heat burnt between them. He pulled her closer, devouring her mouth. She didn't want him to go. She wanted to explore what was between them. Intimately.

These feelings... I don't know how to explain them, but I need you to be safe.

He pulled away, a troubled expression on his face.

"He's not a danger to me, only you. I'll be back."

He released her and strode away. She put a hand to her mouth where she could still feel the ghost of his lips. She backed away, sitting down on the bed.

Why do I care so much about him already?

Putting her head in her hands, she let out a long sigh. Az wasn't just a man, he was an Archangel and he was giving his attention to her. She wasn't sure what she'd done to deserve it. He'd been so dismissive of humans when they'd met. They'd argued countless times, but he'd done nothing but protect her anyway. And now he'd kissed her.

Her phone buzzed in her pocket. She pulled it out, looking down at the screen. Jason. She sighed. She should just get this over with. She hadn't wanted to talk to Jason whilst Azrael was around, but she might as well take the opportunity whilst he was out dealing with Lucifer.

"Hello Jason."

"You've finally answered."

"What do you want?"

"I miss you."

She gritted her teeth. *Funny that. I don't miss you. Not one bit.*

"You should've thought about that before you cheated on me."

"Please, Alice, I just want to talk. Will you meet with me?"

"No."

"Please, I promise I'll do better. I've made a huge mistake."

No kidding.

"I don't have anything to say to you."

"Just one drink, please."

"I can't."

Azrael had told her to stay put. She wasn't about to leave the penthouse when Lucifer was out there. It was the first time he'd left her properly alone since they'd met.

"Then I'll come to you."

"No."

"Alice, just give me a chance."

She closed her eyes, taking a deep breath. Jason wasn't going to take no for an answer.

"Fine."

She gave him the address of a bar nearby before hanging up. Guilt flooded her. She'd told Azrael she wouldn't leave, but what harm would she come to? She'd give Jason ten minutes then she'd come right back.

She went to the wardrobe, pulling out something more appropriate. She changed before putting on a dash of makeup.

I'll show Jason I'm better off without him.

She put her contacts in before she picked up her bag and shrugged on her coat.

Stepping into the lift, she fidgeted.

Az is going to kill me if I get into any trouble.

She wasn't sure why he even cared about her, but his actions spoke louder than words. He told her he wanted to continue what they'd started. He wanted to kiss her again, but did that mean he wanted more? She wasn't sure how she could believe that he, Azrael the Archangel of Death, would want her, a human.

She hurried out of the building before she changed her mind. A few minutes later, she entered the bar. Sitting by himself, his blonde hair messy, blue eyes twinkling, was Jason. She took measured steps towards him. His eyes lit up when he saw her.

"You came," he said.

"Yes."

She sat down next to him. She regretted even coming out. It was a stupid idea.

"You look good."

"Get to the point, Jason."

His expression fell and he sighed.

"I'm sorry."

I feel nothing. His apology is meaningless. Jason isn't who I care for. The man I feel something for isn't here. He's with his brother. Oh, Az, what am I doing?

Chapter Seven

Azrael landed in Hyde Park, the wind whipping around his head. His wings disappeared in the next instant. Standing by the Joy of Life fountain, looking up at the statue was his brother. It had been centuries since they'd seen each other. There was something deadly about the figure in front of him.

"Azrael."

His voice was soft and measured. His dark hair ruffled. His tanned skin reflecting in the glow of the streetlights. He was the Morningstar. Azrael remembered the time when he'd been kind, but the Lucifer before him was a different angel altogether. Twisted by his time ruling over Hell. Locked out of Heaven, just like his brother. It made him long for the days when they'd been brothers in arms, not the strangers they were now.

"Lucifer."

"Earth hasn't been kind to you."

"I could say the same of Hell."

There was a ghost of a smile on Lucifer's lips. Neither of them could deny being away from their home had done them any favours. Lucifer had become angry and dark, whilst Azrael was disillusioned and lonely.

"You found the girl."

Azrael was silent. This was the reason Lucifer was here. The demon had delivered his message. He wished things between them were different, but he knew Lucifer placed part of the blame on him for their exile from Heaven. Azrael knew better. He knew their father had kicked them out for more than just their rebellion against him. It had everything to do with the Darkness and the end.

"And how exactly do you know about her?"

"Did you think I haven't been keeping an eye on you? She's important. He knows you have her. I do wonder if this was part of His plan. Were you meant to find her? I suppose it doesn't matter now."

Lucifer keeping tabs on him wasn't surprising in the slightest. He imagined the King of Hell made sure he knew what all the angels on Earth were up to.

"What is your point?"

He wasn't in the mood for cryptic conversation, but Lucifer was never one for straight talking. Perhaps it would never have come to this if he was. It made no difference. They couldn't change the past. The future was a different matter altogether.

"What did He tell you, Azrael?"

"What makes you think I'm amenable to telling you anything? Hundreds of years and I hear nothing from you. Has Hell really kept you so busy that you couldn't even say hello to your own brother?"

Lucifer turned to him, his dark eyes icy. When had he become so cold? *What has Hell really done to him? Did Father really think forcing his son to punish souls was going to make him any less angry?*

"Hell is none of your concern. Father said it would come, the Darkness. He warned me it would arrive in an unexpected form. She can see us, can she not? All of our glory laid bare at her feet."

There was no point denying such a thing. If Alice was ever to meet Lucifer, she'd see him for what he was.

What did he mean by the Darkness coming in an unexpected form? Was he talking about Alice? Was she at the centre of all of this?

"Again, what is your point?"

"She will bring ruin to us. You should give her to me so I can end it."

He stiffened. He wasn't going to give Alice to his brother even if she was mixed up in this. His chest tightened at the thought. Lucifer wanted to take her away from him. To kill her before the end started. He couldn't even entertain the idea. She was far too important to him.

"No."

Lucifer ignored him, taking a few steps off to the side. His eyes rested on the fountain again. His shoulders were tense, his brow furrowed.

"Do you know what our brothers and sisters decided to do when they discovered His plan? They colluded with demons."

That isn't possible. Angels would never work with demons.

"They've been experimenting with His human creations, trying to give humanity a fighting chance against the Darkness. I hear they succeeded."

"Experiments?"

"Yes, creating beings who possess both demon and angel souls. You should seek them out. I'm told a pair of them live in the city."

He frowned. This was troubling. Why would his brothers and sisters go to such lengths? There had to be more to this. He needed to know why they'd taken this course of action.

"Why are you telling me this?"

"Since you won't give her to me, you've sealed our fate. Even you won't stand by idly when it comes. You might have sided with me against Him, but Father sent you here for a reason. Make no mistake, brother, I will find out what He told you."

Good luck with that. I'm not telling you anything now you've admitted you'll kill her.

Lucifer raised his head to the sky, a smile appearing on his face.

"Oh, Azrael. It seems your human girl isn't as well hidden as you like to think."

And with that, his brother took to the skies. Azrael stood for a moment.

Alice. I told you not to leave.

His wings unfurled and he was airborne. He tried to home in on her, but there were so many humans in this city. The sound of their chatter blared in his head. He growled, soaring towards the penthouse. She couldn't have gone far. He could sense his brother was still on Earth.

If he so much as lays a hand on Alice... I will not hesitate to end him. She is mine. I won't let anyone else have her.

He landed on the roof of his building, balancing on the edge. His wings fluttered in the wind. He felt for her. There was nothing. He cursed. This was the last thing he needed. He'd kept her safe for weeks.

It was Lucifer's fault. If he hadn't called to him, Azrael would be with her now. He'd be touching her in all the places he wanted to. In all the ways he'd imagined. The thought of it stirred his senses. He couldn't hold back any longer. Not when he wanted her like nothing else in this world.

He'd have to deal with what his brother told him later. It troubled him greatly. How was she involved in this? Had it been what his father meant by him bringing the end? Lucifer said she would bring ruin, but he didn't know the last words their father had said to Azrael.

The Darkness will come in an unexpected form.

It couldn't be her, could it? That was ridiculous. Their father would never have hidden the Darkness inside one of his precious human beings.

Unless she is the vessel...

He shook himself. Now was not the time. She was in danger. He tried to listen for her again.

Come on, Alice, think about me. Please.

Moments ticked by, but he could only hear the idle chatter of humanity. He cursed again, wishing she'd listened to him about staying in the penthouse.

"Az..."

That one single thought was all it took. She was so close. He flew straight towards where he'd heard her. A dark alley loomed below him. He rushed down, landing with a thump.

"Get off me," she shouted, struggling with a blonde-haired man.

Azrael frowned taking in the scene.

Who is this trying to assault her? It better not be who I think it is.

"I love you."

"No, you don't."

The man pushed her against the wall, trying to hold Alice still. They hadn't noticed he was there.

"Let go of me, Jason!"

She kicked out at the man, but he managed to narrowly avoid her leg.

"Stop struggling."

This was the cheating ex. She'd been right about one thing. He wasn't worth her tears. Anger burnt in Azrael's chest. Enough was enough. This man needed to be stopped.

"Let her go."

"*Az! Oh... fuck.*"

Jason and Alice looked over at him.

"Who the hell are you?" Jason asked, his eyebrows shooting up in surprise.

"You've made a mistake touching her, Jason."

"How... How do you know my name?"

"*I'm sorry, I'm sorry I left.*"

He could hear her reaching out to him, but his focus was on Jason. He'd been trying to force her. He was in no mood for this. He'd already been interrupted by his brother when all he wanted to do was show Alice exactly how much he desired her. Now, her ex was touching her. There would be little chance of him granting the man mercy at this rate.

"I know a lot about you, mortal."

Jason moved away slightly from Alice before pressing her behind him.

"Stay away from us."

"Funny little man. Do you think you're a match for me?"

"I don't know who you are. This is between me and her."

Alice tried to move away from him, but he reached out, holding her arm in an iron grip.

"Jason, let go of me. You don't want to do this."

Her grey eyes met Azrael's, full of regret. He wasn't angry with her, but with Lucifer and Jason.

She tried to wrench out of her ex's grasp.

"We don't even know you," Jason said. "Mind your own business."

His eyes darkened and narrowed. This human was sorely trying his patience.

"Don't know me? Oh, you're mistaken, young man."

"Jason, please. Stop," Alice said, still trying to tug her arm away. "Just stop."

"*Az, help me.*"

The plea in her mind almost broke him. His irritation with the cheating bastard flared. He put his arms out.

"You asked for this, Jason."

The air shimmered, wings appearing at his back as he donned his angelic armour. Alice's eyes widened to saucers. Smooth metal lay across his chest, covering his legs and arms. A huge sword appeared in his hand. A halo of light glowed softly above his head.

"Oh, holy, shit... You're... Az... Fuck. He's like the most incredible, magnificent being and he's saving me. Oh, heart, please stop pounding so hard! Seeing him hurts my eyes."

Jason dropped Alice's arm, blood draining from his face. He took a step back.

"What... What the fuck are you?" he said, his voice high pitched and squeaky.

"Azrael, the Angel of Death," Alice whispered.

Jason turned to her, eyes wide. His mouth dropped open.

"Angel? Have you lost your mind?"

"No, Jason." She stepped away from him. "You didn't listen to me. I told you we're over and I meant it." She backed away further, towards Azrael. "Stay away from me... from us."

"Wait, you know him?"

She reached Azrael, turning her face up towards him. There was no fear in her expression. Affection, admiration, but not fear.

"Yes. He's my angel."

His heart jolted at her words. Her angel. He supposed he was. He'd tried to keep her safe. And he wanted to make her his.

No, she is mine already. I'm going to make sure she knows it.

"Alice... What the fuck have you got yourself wrapped up in? Do you really expect me to believe he's an angel?"

"She doesn't expect anything from you. She has me," Azrael said. "She told me what you did. You don't deserve her."

He wrapped an arm around her, pulling her close. The sword in his hand disappeared. He cupped her cheek. She was safe. He'd reached her before Lucifer.

"You're... Let her go!"

"Az, take me home, please," she whispered.

He turned his head towards Jason one last time.

"If you come near her again, I will not hesitate to break you, human."

"Alice, you cannot expect me to believe you want to go with him? Is this where you've been all this time? With... with an angel?"

Alice huddled closer to him, resting her cheek on the metal plate of his armour.

"Yes. This is where I've been, with him," she said.

"Where I belong. I can't breathe without you near me."

"Alice," he whispered. "This isn't a conversation we should have with an audience. We'll talk about it at the penthouse."

She nodded against his chest.

"Alice, please, you can't be serious," Jason said.

She turned to him.

"I'm perfectly serious. I don't want to see you again. We're done. I think we were over long before I even moved here. I was stupid enough to think you cared, but you never did. The only person you care about is yourself. Don't ever contact me again."

She looked back up at Azrael. Her eyes bright with unshed tears. It tore at him. Jason hadn't treated her right. He hadn't seen what was in front of him. A girl who deserved so much more. He was determined to be her everything.

"Alice!"

Neither of them looked at Jason. Azrael wrapped his other arm around her, taking off into the skies. Alice's face buried in his shoulder. He could feel her crying softly.

Alice. Sweet, innocent, Alice. I will burn for you.

Chapter Eight

*A*lice couldn't stop the tears flowing. She clutched him tighter, the wind rushing around her ears. Tonight was one huge mess.

Stupid, stupid, stupid.

"You're not calling me stupid, are you?" he asked.

"No," she sobbed. "Quit listening."

She wanted one private thought to herself. Despite how she felt about the angel, she still hated him hearing her when she didn't want him to.

"It's hard not to, but I'll try for you."

He'd try for her?

She wanted to look at him, but she didn't want him seeing her tear streaked face. She was sure her makeup was running everywhere.

This is so embarrassing. I hope he doesn't think I'm crying over him or anything.

She was upset with herself and Jason. Mostly herself for being an idiot and going to see him. She wanted to have a clean break, but he'd tried to get her to go home with him. It had been fine until they'd gotten outside and he'd dragged her into that alley.

She felt her feet set down on the pavement for a moment before Azrael swept an arm under her legs and picked her up.

"Az!"

He ignored her and carried her into the building, straight into the lift. He punched in the code with her still in his arms. The door closed. She was thankful there was no one else in here. When they reached the penthouse, he set her down. She didn't look at him as she hurried away towards the bedroom.

"Alice?"

He followed her, but she couldn't stop. She ran into the bathroom, shutting the door behind her. She flipped the lock. It wouldn't keep him out, but she needed a minute. She put both hands on the counter next to the sink, looking at her face. Her mascara was running, her makeup streaked across her face with her tears. She tugged her makeup wipes towards her and wiped it away until her face was clear.

"Alice, open the door."

She sighed, throwing the wipe in the bin before going over to the door. She opened it. He stood there, in full armour. She looked up into his bright green eyes. He was still glowing. Everything about the angel in front of her made her heart ache. He reached out, cupping her face.

"What were you doing?"

She looked at her hands.

"Honestly, I didn't want you to see me looking like a mess after I'd been crying."

He ran a thumb across her bottom lip. It made her skin tingle and caused a stirring in her stomach. Her eyes went to his mouth.

"Why would you think that would bother me?"

"Because you've told me you don't like it when humans cry on you and you don't like human emotions."

"I wanted to kiss your tears away."

Her heart skipped a beat.

He wants to what?

She raised her eyes to his just in time to see him lean towards her. His mouth met hers, his arms coming around her. The cold metal of his armour dug into her chest. All her focus was on his mouth, gently pressing against hers. He really did know how to kiss a girl. *I can't be the only human he's kissed, right?*

He backed them away from the bathroom, into the bedroom. She didn't quite register what was happening until she felt her back hit a wall. His fingers roamed down her sides. He pushed her coat off her shoulders. He released her mouth to press kisses down her jaw and the column of her throat. She couldn't breathe.

"Alice," he whispered. "I want to kiss you, to feel you."

He was answering her question from earlier. *He wants this? He wants... me?* How could she even believe that after all of his ranting about mortals? She put her hands on his chest, pushing him back. His eyes were questioning when he looked down at her.

"I can't do this right now. Also, you're all in like serious battle gear and it's just weird."

She hadn't meant to say that last part. She didn't want him to think she didn't like his attention, but her head was a mess. He stepped away from her, looking down at his armour for a moment.

"I don't really know what's going on between us," she continued. "All you've done is tell me how much you dislike humans."

She ran a hand through her hair. She hadn't meant to start this line of conversation.

"I'm sorry I went out to see Jason. I thought it would get him to stop contacting me, but he had other ideas. Him touching me, makes me feel sick and now you're kissing me and it's just confusing. I need... I need time alone to think, process what's going on."

He looked back up at her.

"Time..."

"Yes, time."

He frowned.

Not forever, Az... just like... an hour?

"You told me not to listen to your thoughts."

She shrugged. It was kind of becoming a habit to talk to him in her head. It was sometimes easier than admitting things out loud.

"I'm going to go in there." She pointed at the bathroom. "I don't want you to think I'm going to leave again. I know it's not safe and, well, I want to stay here." *With you. Only with you because my heart races when you're near me.*

She wasn't sure if he'd listened to the last part. He didn't object when she slipped away. Going into the bathroom, she left the door ajar, hoping it would be enough for him to know she wasn't trying to shut him out.

She ran herself a bubble bath. She took her contact lenses out, throwing the daily disposables in the bin. She only needed them and her glasses to see things at a distance. She undressed, leaving her clothes in a neat pile on the counter before slipping into the water. She lay back, the bubbles settling around her. Staring out at the London skyline, the lights twinkling, she tried to relax. It was beautiful seeing the city this way.

Since she'd seen the bath the first day she'd been here, she'd wanted to try it out. It was huge. *Can definitely fit more than one person in here.* She flushed as she imagined taking a bath with him. She shook herself. She'd come in here to get away from her thoughts about the angel, not to fantasise about him.

She put her arms on the side of the bath, laying her head across them as she stared out at the dark sky. *I was an idiot to go see Jason.* She wished she'd just stayed here like Az had told her to. She wondered what happened with Lucifer. Did he find out what the Devil wanted with her? The Devil who was really an Archangel himself. *Is Lucifer as beautiful as Azrael? Are all angels beautiful?*

She cursed herself. Why was she even thinking about that? Her thoughts were filled with his perfect features. She wanted to see him, in all his glory. Groaning, she tipped her head back against the lip of the bath, putting a hand over her eyes. She needed to get a grip. He probably didn't even really want her at all. How could he? He was the epitome of perfection and she was nothing. Even though his personality was occasionally prickly, he still managed to show her that he had a softer side.

There's something about him which is just so sad. He's been alone all this time. It makes my heart hurt, ache for him.

He couldn't go home. His real home was no longer an option for him.

"An hour is far too long."

She looked up, startled before sinking into the bubbles to hide her nakedness from him. He strode into the room, dressed in a white t-shirt and a long pair of trousers. His feet were bare.

"Um... you do realise I'm not wearing anything in here, don't you?"

"And?"

She flushed, scowling at him. He went over to the window, shoving his hands in his pockets, staring out at the skyline.

"And... it's kind of not cool to watch me bathing."

"I won't look."

She stared at his back. His broad shoulders and the line of his narrow hips.

Oh my. It's not just the water making me feel hot right now.

"You should voice it out loud if it's really how I make you feel."

She sunk lower in the water, pressing her hands to her cheeks.

"I can't control my thoughts."

"And yet you asked me to stop when it's clear I want to give you what you desire."

"What?"

"You want me to touch you, intimately. I've heard it enough times in your head."

She couldn't quite believe he'd just said that.

The ground needs to swallow me whole, right now. I'm going to die of sheer mortification and embarrassment.

She couldn't exactly deny it. He wouldn't believe her if she tried. She needed to change the subject and fast.

"Did you see your brother?"

His back stiffened. She ached to get out and hold him, to melt away the tension radiating off her angel. *Okay, I might have told Jason he's my angel, but he's not really mine, is he?*

"Yes."

"You don't want to talk about it."

"No."

"Did you at least find out what he wants with me?"

"In a sense."

She frowned. Why would he want her company when he wasn't being particularly communicative? He turned away from the window, his eyes on hers.

"I will deal with Lucifer. I'm more concerned about keeping you away from him. You're not safe."

"Why, does he want me dead or something?"

There was a flicker of worry in his eyes for the slightest moment. She had been joking, but the seriousness of his expression made her pause.

"Wait... that is what he wants."

"Alice..."

She sat up, forgetting she was naked for a moment. She crossed her arms over her chest, hiding her breasts from him. His eyes blazed. He strode across the room and knelt down beside the bath. He reached out and cupped her face.

"Don't be embarrassed to show yourself to me."

How can I not be?

"Why not?" she whispered.

"I want to see you."

"But why? I don't understand."

"Do you think I don't desire you, Alice?"

Her face burnt brighter.

"No, how could you? You're an angel and I'm a human."

His eyes searched hers for a moment. Without warning, he got to his feet and stepped into the bath with her. He knelt before her, in between her legs, still in all of his clothes. She stared up at him in confusion.

"What are you doing?"

He took her hands, tugging them away from her breasts. He looked her over, his eyes blazing with want, need. He pinned her hands to the back of the bath before leaning over her.

"I have been on Earth for centuries, never once have I felt desire until I met you. I want you, Alice. I want to touch you, to feel your body against mine, to be inside you. I'm burning for you and only you. Am I making myself clear?"

She nodded. The intensity of his gaze and his words left no room for doubt. His eyes fell to her breasts. His tongue darted out, running over his bottom lip. When his eyes met hers again, she felt frozen in place by the desire reflecting in them.

"Do you want this? Do you want me?"

She bit her lip, utterly exposed to him at that moment.

"I think you know I do."

"I want to hear you say it out loud."

"I want you."

He let go of her hands, running one down the column of her throat. His fingers roamed lower until he cupped her breast, his thumb running over the nipple. She gasped. He leant down, taking the other in his mouth. His tongue swirled over the sensitive nub.

"Oh... fuck."

Am I seeing stars right now? His mouth... oh, if that's what he can do to my breasts, what about...?

She could feel him smiling against her skin. It was going to make for an interesting experience if he could hear her every thought. Would she even need to tell him what she wanted?

His tongue continued to swirl around her nipple. The jolts running down her skin were intense. His other hand ran down her stomach, dipping below the level of the water. His fingers brushed up her inner thigh. She jerked in surprise.

Whoa... What...

They met her softness, parting her so he could access her core. His fingers brushed over the nub, circling it gently. She was going to combust on the spot.

Oh, oh, what are you doing to me?

"I'm going to make you come."

Hearing him say that was just about the hottest thing she'd ever heard in her life. Her very own Archangel wanted to make her come. He raised his head, staring down at her for a moment before he kissed her.

She cupped his face with one hand, the other on his shoulder, nails digging into the hard muscle. His fingers were like magic. Her breathing came hard and heavy.

She had to pull away from his mouth for a moment to groan. She felt it building inside her. The explosive end that was to come. He placed kisses to her neck before his tongue curled around her ear. His breath hot against it.

"Hearing you moan is making me hard for you."

Do you want to fuck me?

"Is that what you want me to call it?"

Only if you want to. I mean... I haven't heard you swear before.

"So, if I told you I want to fuck you until you're screaming my name... that would be acceptable?"

She couldn't reply. Hearing him say that sent her over the edge. She cried out, trembling as her climax rocked through her. Her fingers dug harder into his shoulder. Stars blurred her vision. Her body shook uncontrollably, all her limbs felt like jelly. The intense waves of pleasure took her under and drowned her. Nothing and no one had ever made her come so hard and with such intensity.

Azrael... whatever you did to me, I want you to do it again and more.

Chapter Nine

Alice panted, coming down from the clouds. His touch was electrifying on so many levels. His mouth found hers again, locking her lips in a searing kiss. She wrapped her arms around his neck, pulling him down towards her.

His clothes were thoroughly wet, but he didn't seem to mind. She felt his solid chest against hers. She wanted to see him. All of him. She ran her hands down his back until they latched onto the edge of his t-shirt, but he put a hand on hers to stop her.

"Not yet, Alice."

She stared up into his green eyes, confusion marring her features.

"I thought you..."

"Wanted you? Yes, but not tonight. You need sleep."

His hands ran down her sides. He tucked them under her behind. He picked her up with him, stepping out of the bath. They were both dripping wet. She slid down him, where she could feel how much he wanted her before her feet hit the ground. He held her away from him, his eyes roaming down the length of her. Her face burnt.

He gets to see all of me, touch all of me. How is that fair? All I want is to see him, be close to him.

She couldn't look at him as he made her sit on the edge of the bath. He leant down, whipping the plug out.

"You only have to ask."

"For the last time, stop that."

"Alice, what do you want to see? I'll give you what you want, just tell me. Don't you know I want to make you happy?"

"I want the ground to swallow me up because I'm mortified having this conversation with you."

When she dared look at him, he was kneeling in front of her with a towel, smiling.

Did he just say he wants to make me happy? I'm not going crazy, am I?

"Would it make it easier if I did this?"

He clicked his fingers and then he was dry and only clad in boxers. She couldn't breathe. Seeing him was more than she could take. She gripped the edge of the bath, her knuckles going white.

Oh. My. Eyes. He is the epitome of perfection.

"I take it from your reaction, you're not displeased."

"How could I ever be?" she whispered. "It almost hurts to look at you."

He stood, wrapping the towel around her. Her face was level with his stomach. Tentatively, she reached out, brushing her fingers against his soft skin. He tensed for a moment, sucking in a breath. She snatched her hand back, guilt flooding her.

Did I go too far?

"No. It was unexpected, not unpleasant."

He cupped her face, leaning down to kiss her, his mouth soft and warm against hers. He pulled away and began drying her thoroughly.

"You don't have to do that, you know."

"I want to take care of you, especially after that worthless excuse for a mortal put his hands on you."

There was the angel she knew, disparaging humans again.

"For someone who doesn't like humans, you're being awfully nice to this one."

"Would you rather I go back to lumping you in with all the other inane mortals I've encountered?"

She grinned.

"I was only teasing."

"Hmm... Is that the only teasing you had in mind?"

She spluttered as he scooped her up in his arms, towel and all, and carried her into the bedroom. He set her down on the bed and pulled a few things out of the wardrobe before insisting on dressing her.

"Is me being naked too distracting?" she asked.

"Yes."

Does he really find me that attractive? I mean he said he desires me, wants to be in me... And the way he touched me... I have to take him at his word.

"I'm not the one who said I needed sleep."

He pulled back the covers and settled her down before tucking them around her. He made to leave when she reached out and held his hand.

"Where are you going?"

"Your rules about the bed still stand."

She frowned. *Rules? Oh, shit.*

"I made those up because I was unsure of what your intentions towards me were. I want you here with me."

She tugged his hand, pulling him down towards her. He came willingly. She pulled back the covers. He tucked her up in his arms, her face pressed to his chest. Warmth spread through her. She ran her fingers down his side, enjoying the sensation of his skin on hers.

"Go to sleep."

So bossy. Alice, you have to stay with me. Alice, don't leave the penthouse. Alice, I demand you let me see you naked. Alice, I'm going to make you scream. Alice, I won't have sex with you because you need to sleep.

She flushed when she realised what she'd thought. Daring not to look at his face, she buried hers deeper into his chest.

"I'll leave if you don't," he said.

He so heard that. Even if he's choosing to ignore me.

"If you don't want me to touch you, perhaps you should put a shirt on."

He flattened her hand on his side before moving it lower until her fingers met the top of his boxers. She hesitated when he took his hand away and looked up at him. There was a hint of a challenge in his eyes. She could feel her face burning.

Does he want me to touch him... there?

He said nothing, merely regarding her, his lip curled up at the side. She swallowed. He'd told her to go to sleep and yet he was challenging her to touch him, intimately. Was this his response to her little outburst in her head about how demanding he was?

She moved her hand, gently pressing down as she shifted over him, straddling his legs. She leant over towards his face, feeling a little bold.

"What is it you want me to do, Az?"

"Whatever you wish."

She ran her fingernails down his chest.

"I think you have something in mind."

His green eyes glinted with mischief. She replaced her fingers with her lips, looking up at him. His hands curled around her legs, fingertips brushing against her skin.

Have I told you how I've longed to touch you?

"Without words, yes."

His body was solid, warm, chiselled to perfection. It wasn't just his appearance which drew her in. He seemed so adrift in this world. She'd felt the same disconnection from her surroundings, almost as if going through the motions without really feeling anything at all. Being with Azrael set everything alight.

She shifted lower, kissing the hard muscle of his stomach. When she met the waistband of his boxers, she eyed him again. His lips were parted, breath coming faster. His eyes shut, a little furrow in his brow. *Wait... he really is enjoying what I'm doing.* The sight of him made her heart pound.

"Alice... don't stop," he whispered.

She hooked her fingers into the waistband before she tugged them down. He moved to let her take his boxers off. When she looked at him, her breath caught in her throat. *Oh, wow.* She bit her lip. She tentatively reached out and touched him. He tensed, his eyes squeezing shut further. She ran her fingers down the length of him. When he didn't ask her to stop, she made up her mind.

Not sure this is what you wanted, but I hope I make you feel good.

He opened his eyes just as she leant down and took him in her mouth, her hand wrapped around the base.

"Alice," he hissed.

She could see his fists clenching and unclenching at his sides. She moved at a steady pace, her free hand reaching out to take one of his. He entwined their fingers together, staring down at her with hazy eyes. His other hand curled into her hair, encouraging her to continue.

She increased her pace. His fingers tightened in hers before he groaned. Somehow, she knew it was genuine pleasure and not some show he was putting on for her. He was always in control, but right now, she had him in the palm of her hand.

My beautiful angel. I want to be the balm to your suffering.

"You are," he murmured, his voice so quiet she thought she'd imagined it.

He looked so unguarded, vulnerable almost. It made her heart ache with an intensity she'd never experienced before. She wanted to take his pain away. All of it. She could feel him twitching. His mouth opened and closed with each breath. His fingers tightened in her hair, pressing her down. She took more, wanting to give him what he needed. When she felt him pulsate, over and over, she knew he'd let go entirely.

"Alice," he growled.

He released her hair, his hand dropping back on the bed. She sat up.

Well, no mess with angels... apparently.

She heard him chuckle.

"Humans have too many bodily fluids."

"And you don't."

He shook his head. His eyes were still closed.

"I'm not supposed to do such things with humans, but when He stranded me here, I stopped caring about Heaven's rules."

"I see."

He tugged her towards him. He held her to his chest, stroking her hair.

"I went through the motions with others, but it was for them, not me."

I don't like the thought of him with other women, but he's lived such a long time, it's not as if I can be jealous.

"And with me?"

"Oh, I think what you just did was most definitely for me."

Was he teasing her? Didn't he realise how self-conscious she was about this whole thing? All she wanted was for him to genuinely enjoy it. To give him pleasure just as he'd given her.

"Az... did you actually like that? Don't say yes to make me feel better. I want the truth."

He opened his eyes. They were glittering in the low light.

"You have a magic mouth."

She scowled.

"I'm serious, Alice."

He cupped her cheek. She was suddenly assaulted with a stream of consciousness.

"*She is so sweet. If that's what she can do to me with her mouth... I want to feel her body, her sex, her everything. Touching her soft, delicate skin drives me crazy. I don't know why I feel this way, but she's a beacon, calling me to her. Sweet, innocent Alice. I am burning for you.*"

She blinked rapidly when he released her face. He was smiling, his eyes full of admiration.

"That's how you feel?"

"Yes and more."

She kissed his chest, curling her hand around the back of his head and running her fingers through his hair. She wasn't sure what else to say. A feeling of contentment washed over her. She dropped off to sleep, safe in her angel's arms.

Alice stretched when she awoke but found the bed empty. She frowned, looking around the room. He was nowhere to be seen. She shuffled into the bathroom, brushing her teeth and going about her business. *So glad it's Saturday. No work.* She snagged her glasses, putting them on before picking up her phone and firing off a quick message to Chris.

You were right about everything. He kissed me last night.

The response was almost immediate.

Holy fuckballs. How was it? Please tell me it was amazing. I can't even imagine what it'd be like.

Euphoric. Did a little more than just kissing.

Tell me all right now!

I need to go find him. I'll call later, promise.

Alice! You dare leave me hanging?!

She laughed, putting her phone down. A part of her wanted to ring Chris and tell him everything, but then Az would hear their conversation.

She walked towards the living room, pausing in the doorway. Standing with his back to her, staring down at the city below was Azrael. He was topless, only clad in a pair of shorts. Her mouth dried up.

She tiptoed into the room, curling her arms around him and resting her cheek on his back. He stiffened for a moment before the tension in his body evaporated.

"Sneaking up on an angel is a bad idea."

"As if you didn't hear me."

"I thought you'd sleep longer. Did I not wear you out?"

She snorted.

It'd take a lot more than that to tire me out.

"I was missing an angel."

"Oh? And which one would that be? There are thousands."

"This one," she whispered, tightening her arms around him.

"Mmm, come here."

She let go of him before coming around his side. Without warning, he pinned her to the window, green eyes glittering with amusement. Her pulse spiked.

One look from him and I'm melting on the spot.

"What were you looking at?" she asked.

"Now or when you came in?"

"Before I interrupted you."

"Lucifer hasn't returned to Hell. I was thinking."

She curled her hands around his back, her fingers dancing over his smooth skin. His muscles twitched at the contact. The way he said it made it seem as though it was unusual for Lucifer to remain on Earth.

"Why does he want me dead?"

His eyes darkened, the tension in his muscles returning. She could feel it radiating off him and regretted asking the question.

"He thinks you're a part of something much larger going on."

"You're not going to let him kill me, are you?"

His eyes widened for a moment before he frowned.

"Why would you even ask that?"

Isn't it obvious?

"He's your brother."

"Do you think that gives him the right to take you from me?"

That was the last thing she thought. She just wasn't sure how close the two of them were now. He'd said he'd not spoken to Lucifer in a long time, but it didn't mean he didn't care about his brother any longer.

"Well, no."

"I sense a but here."

"Az, I don't understand why I'm so important."

"To him or to me?"

"In all of this, whatever this situation is." She waved a hand around. "Like a few weeks ago, I was a normal girl and now... now, there's you, Lucifer wants me dead and I know there's shit you're not telling me about. It scares me. All of it, but especially this, right here, between us."

His eyes grew wary.

"We don't really know much about each other. Yet... and yet... when I look at you, I see all your loneliness, the disconnection, the years of suffering and it all feels so real to me."

He reached up, holding her face in his hands.

"I'm the only one who can see you for what you really are, aren't I? That's why Jason didn't believe me."

"Yes," was all he said in response.

"Is that why you want me?"

His hands on her face tightened, his eyes growing dark.

"You know that's not why. Can't you accept I want you for you?"

"I can try."

It was all she could do. It was hard to understand why an immortal being would want to be with her, a plain human.

He kissed her, their mouths melding together. The temperature between them spiked. His fingers curled into her short hair, holding her still. She could drown in him. Right here. Right now.

Distracting me with kisses isn't fair.

"Were we not done?" he asked, pulling away enough to allow her to breathe again.

"No. I talked, you didn't."

She wasn't quite sure if he didn't want to have this conversation or he just didn't know what to say.

"Lucifer won't get to you."

"I meant about us."

He pulled away further, dropping his hands from her face. He looked off to the side, eyes full of caution.

"It is disconcerting having you see all of those things."

"You mean..."

"My suffering as you call it."

"I feel lonely and adrift too. I was trying to say I sort of understand, in my own way."

He ran a hand through his auburn hair. She was momentarily distracted by it glinting in the sunlight.

"I didn't realise you were one for deep conversations first thing in the morning."

"I'm sorry, it wasn't my intention."

She pressed herself to him, her cheek resting against his bare chest, glasses a little askew.

"Would it be so hard not to question this? To let it be what it is."

He had made his feelings towards her clear. He wanted her and she wanted him too. Was there any need to keep trying to work out the whys and hows? Did it really matter?

"I guess not."

"When things are clearer, I'll tell you what I know about Lucifer and our Father. I want to be sure. Do you understand?"

"Yes."

She clutched him tighter, her fingers digging into his back. He kissed the top of her head, leaning his chin on it.

"I'm going to need you to get dressed now. We have some people to track down."

Chapter Ten

They stepped into a dingy bar. The paint peeled off the walls. The wooden furniture dark. She kept close to the angel, not wanting to catch the eye of any of the patrons. This didn't seem like a very upmarket place and it certainly wasn't the type of bar she'd ever imagine Az going into. He stuck out like a sore thumb. He wore a navy suit like the first time they'd met. Az always looked immaculate and put together.

"Why are we here?" she whispered.

"The vampire bar we went to isn't open yet. This is where the animals amongst us like to frequent."

"You mean like werewolves?"

"Yes, but many of them change into different creatures."

The bartender, a man with sandy brown hair, looked them up and down with a frown. Standing next to him was a blonde girl. She was looking over at a red-haired man sitting on a stool on the other side of the bar.

"Well, that's different," Azrael said.

"What is?"

"That girl. Bitten, not born, and pregnant."

Alice looked at the girl intently. She was most definitely pregnant. Her t-shirt, with the words 'The Werehouse' in stark white writing, stretched over her stomach.

"What is she?"

"A panther. Her child will be one too."

She wasn't about to ask how he knew that. As an angel, he could see things humans couldn't. He hadn't exactly told her all about his full capabilities, but perhaps he'd explain things more now they were together. Sort of.

Are we together? Is this a thing? What do I even call us? I mean he's an angel. Do they even have relationships like humans amongst themselves?

Azrael took her hand, entwining their fingers together and tugged her over to the bar. She couldn't help wondering if he'd heard her or not.

"Hello, what can I get you?" the girl said, smiling.

She was very pretty. Alice couldn't imagine this girl turning into a panther.

"I am looking for information," Azrael replied.

"Oh. Um, Gareth, do you want to handle this?"

The sandy-haired man's eyes narrowed.

"What exactly do you want?"

Azrael rolled his eyes, leaning towards Alice. His lips brushed against her ear sending a tingle down her spine.

"Not sure we're welcome here."

"There's no harm asking. Though, you didn't even tell me who you want to find."

He turned back to the bartender and the girl.

"I'm looking for two people who are half angel and half demon."

The sandy-haired man's eyebrows shot up. The red-haired man looked at them in surprise.

"Half angel, half demon? I didn't know that was possible. Are you sure?"

"Would I be asking otherwise?"

She could see the frustration in Azrael's expression. She didn't think he liked having to ask for help. Why was he looking for these people?

"Does this have something to do with your meeting with you know who last night?" she asked.

"Yes," he replied.

"Look, I don't know anyone like that," the sandy-haired man the girl had called Gareth said.

"I know someone we can ask," the girl piped up.

Gareth glared at the girl for a moment.

"Izzy, we don't even know who this is."

"Fine, who are you two?" she said, directing her gaze at Alice and Azrael.

"My name is Azrael, but she is none of your concern."

The red-haired man coughed loudly, spluttering.

"What? You can't be serious," he said.

"What's up with you, Evan?" Izzy asked.

"You're an Archangel."

Izzy and Gareth turned back to them, eyes wide.

"An angel?"

Azrael rolled his eyes. Alice hid a smile behind her hand. He really didn't like anyone recognising him.

I bet you regret telling them who you are.

He scowled at her.

"Mortals," he muttered.

"Yes, that's correct," Alice said. "You said you know someone."

"Yes," Izzy said, slowly. "My friend. Hang on."

She turned away, pulling out her phone. Gareth put a hand on her arm.

"Are you sure about this?"

"I'm sick of our communities being so secretive. You know all that shit wouldn't have happened to me if we just shared information. I'm sure."

She moved away further down the bar. Alice wondered what the girl had meant by that. Did it have something to do with her being bitten? Having an Archangel around had its perks. He could tell her things about people no one else would know. She wasn't going to think about the other reasons she wanted Azrael around.

No. Can't think about kissing him and his hands on my body. No. Not helping.

She glanced at him, but he wasn't paying attention to her.

"Why are you with a human?" Gareth asked, turning back to them.

Azrael narrowed his eyes. Alice put a hand on his arm. She could understand their reluctance to help two people they didn't know. She felt him relax under her touch.

"He's protecting me."

"You didn't have to answer for me."

She looked up at him, startled. Since when had he started talking to her in her head? She'd ask him about it later.

"Protecting a human? Aren't you responsible for death?" the red-haired man who recognised Azrael's name asked.

"Do you think I kill everyone I come into contact with?" Azrael replied, his muscles tensing again.

"Whoa, no... I was just curious. Heck, I never thought I'd meet an actual angel."

"I can quite easily make you forget you ever saw me."

Az, cut it out. We didn't come here to fight with these men.

"They're not just men, Alice. They're werewolves."

"Wait a second, how did you know that?" Gareth asked.

"Nothing escapes my notice, wolf."

Alice squeezed his arm. They all needed to calm down. Riling up the werewolves wouldn't get them anywhere.

Enough of the pissing match. If you don't cut it out, there'll be no kissing later.

He turned to her slowly, a sneer forming on his lips. Threatening him with that was definitely not her brightest idea.

"I think you'll find I will be deciding when you get kissed again. I'm in two minds about taking you outside right now."

She swallowed, unsure if she'd enjoy what he had in mind or not.

"So, my friend knows who you're talking about," Izzy said.

Both of them turned to the pregnant werepanther.

"He said your best bet is to go to Fright Night and ask Neave about Ella and Lukas. That's what Alistair said their names are."

"Thank you," Alice said. "Um, congratulations by the way. When is your baby due?"

"In a couple of months," Izzy replied, smiling.

"So, uh, Az said it'll be like you, in case you were wondering."

"Oh. She will?"

"Yes," Azrael said. "Her father is full-blooded, is he not?"

Izzy's eyes widened.

"Yes... Wow. You really are an angel."

"Yeah, he is, but you know, we probably should leave now. Thanks again," Alice said before Azrael had a chance to lay into any of them further.

She tugged on his arm, waving at the three shifters. Azrael let her lead him out of the bar.

A little way down the street, he pulled her into an alley.

"Az…"

His eyes glittered in the sunlight.

"I'm going to punish you for that threat."

"Punish me? What? Why?"

He didn't reply, merely capturing her up in his arms and catapulting them both into the sky, wings fluttering in the wind.

She didn't know whether to be nervous, terrified or excited by the prospect of punishment.

She'd spent the rest of the day on tenterhooks, wondering when he would exact this so-called punishment. By the time they were outside Fright Night again after evening had fallen, she was all but sure he hadn't meant it.

They walked down the steps together and into the bar. It was relatively busy with it being Saturday night. Azrael wrapped an arm around her waist, keeping her pinned to his side.

"Wouldn't want you getting lost," he whispered in her ear.

It sent shivers down her spine. He'd barely touched her when they got back to the penthouse. She most definitely wanted his hands on her. All she could think about was what he'd done to her in the bath last night.

"As if you'd allow me out of your sight again after yesterday."

"You're right. You called yourself my prisoner. I wonder if you feel the same way now."

She didn't reply. He knew the answer to that. He muscled in between a few people at the bar, tucking her under his arm. She wrapped her arms around him. His eyes met hers, heat burning in those green depths.

Why, Az… do you perhaps find it distracting having me pressed up against you?

"Strike two, Alice."

"What? What did I do?"

"Threatening, teasing… You'll see what happens soon enough."

"Oh, it's you two again."

Both of them turned at the sound of the newcomer's voice. It was the same woman who'd served them last time. The one Azrael had said was a vampire. She was half glad her conversation with Az had been interrupted. She dreaded to think what would happen on strike three. Did he have a three strike rule?

"You remember us?" Alice asked.

"Yes, the girl whose boyfriend cheated on her and you're... well, I don't really know what you are other than not being human, that much I can tell."

"Are you Neave?" Azrael asked.

"Yes, I own the bar. What can I do for you?"

"May we speak in private? I have some questions."

Neave looked them over for a moment. She rolled her eyes before calling out to the other two bartenders.

"Back in a bit, business to attend to."

She nodded to the door in the far corner.

"We'll go somewhere quieter."

Azrael tugged Alice along, diving through the crowd. They met Neave at the door marked 'Staff Only' and followed her through it. She led them into the Manager's office. She sat down in a chair behind a large desk, waving a hand at the seats.

"What can I do for you?" she asked.

Alice sat down, but Azrael stood behind her, a hand resting on her shoulder.

"I'll get to the point. My name is Azrael. I'm looking for Ella and Lukas. The two who are half angel and half demon."

Neave eyed him for a moment.

"Why do you want them?"

She didn't seem suspicious, merely curious.

"I wish to speak to them about their origins. It is important."

"Well, I do know them, but as for getting in contact with them, I'd have to ask Daisy."

"And she would be?"

"Oh, the boss' wife who also happens to be Ella's best friend."

"Boss?" Alice asked without thinking.

"Oh, sorry, I always forget to introduce myself properly. I'm second in command of this territory, London. My boss, Gavin, rules the vampires in the area."

She had no idea vampires were so organised, but Azrael hadn't exactly told her much about the world of the supernatural. She looked up at him. He nodded at her.

"I'm aware of their hierarchy, but I do not keep tabs on who is who," he said.

"Can I ask how you knew my name?" Neave said.

"We visited The Werehouse. A panther by the name of Izzy got in touch with someone named Alistair who told her we should speak to you. I grow weary of this little goose chase, but if you would be amenable to contacting your boss' wife..."

Neave shrugged, pulling out her phone. She dialled a number.

"All right, boss. Daisy with you? Um, well, I have some people who need to speak to her friends. Who? Says his name is Azrael... What, you've heard of him?"

The shadows in the corner of the room seemed to shift. The next moment, out stepped a man with brown hair and glasses along with a dark-haired woman in his arms.

Neave ended the call, rolling her eyes and popping the phone on the desk. The woman stepped towards Alice, a smile appearing on her face. Azrael's hand tightened on her shoulder.

"Hello, I'm Daisy, it's nice to meet you."

She stuck her hand out to Alice who shook it.

"Alice... that's Az, I mean Azrael."

The man stared at the two of them, his expression inscrutable. Was this Neave's boss? Daisy looked back at him, rolling her eyes.

"So, my husband didn't exactly say why we're all here."

"Oh, we're looking for Ella and Lukas, Neave said you know them."

"Well, yeah, but what do you need with them?"

Alice looked up at Azrael, expecting him to explain since she didn't really know herself.

"He is an angel, love. I imagine that's why he wants to speak to them. Is it not?" Daisy's husband said.

"An angel? Ella said they weren't supposed to interfere in her life."

The room was silent for a long moment. Alice didn't know if Azrael wanted to reveal his exile from Heaven to these people.

"We just want a conversation with them, nothing more," Alice said, unable to stand the uncomfortable atmosphere.

Daisy whipped out her phone and fired off a series of messages. She stared down at her phone when she got a response.

"Ella says sure, but tomorrow. Anywhere, in particular, you want to meet them?"

"My penthouse will be adequate. Alice, take her number," Azrael said.

Alice handed Daisy her phone for a moment.

"Thank you for your time."

"Hold on," Gavin said. "Why are you seeking them out?"

"The reason they were created. It is coming. If you know who I am, then you know I bring death to the world."

"Okay, this shit is getting weird. What is going on?" Daisy asked.

Alice stood, putting a hand on Azrael's arm.

"He's the Archangel of Death and there's something going down with Heaven, Hell and Earth. I guess you could say your friends are involved in it too. Is that right, Az?"

"You could put it that way."

He smiled at her. She hadn't been very eloquent, but she was pretty sure Azrael was done with the company of other people now. His reluctance to talk much spoke volumes.

"Thank you for putting us in touch with them."

"You're welcome," Daisy said.

Gavin looked like he wanted to say more, but Alice tugged the angel out of the door and back through the bar. She wasn't sure what that was all about, but it seemed best she got Azrael home.

He stood, shuffling his feet when they reached the top of the steps.

"Had enough of other people?" she asked.

"Tiresome inane questions from mortals."

"I hope that's not directed at me."

He stepped towards her, cupping her face with one hand.

"No, never you."

She felt a wave of happiness surge through her. Her heart thumped erratically in her chest.

"So... am I the only exception to your dislike of mortals?"

"Yes."

"I must be special then."

His lip curled up at the side.

"I think I need to show you just how special you are to me."

He tugged her into his arms before she had time to question what that entailed.

Chapter Eleven

*I*nstead of going back to the penthouse, Azrael shot higher in the sky until they were above the clouds. He set them down on top of a particularly large one. Alice looked at their feet, eyes wide with confusion.

"How are we standing on a cloud? Wait... more to the point, why are we here?"

He wasn't quite sure Alice would approve of all his reasons for bringing her up here. It was selfish. Part of him wanted to make their first time memorable for her, but the other half wanted to say 'fuck you' to dear old dad. Taking the final step with her where they were in full view of Heaven. The darker side of him relished the prospect.

"Have you forgotten who I am again?"

"No, I just didn't realise this was possible."

The moon glinted off the clouds, setting off her skin in the low light. He was done waiting. She was going to have a lesson in what it meant to be desired by an angel. He hooked his fingers into her coat, tugging it off her. Next, he began unbuttoning her blouse.

"What... What are you doing?"

"Undressing you."

"Undressing... What? Why?"

She put her hands on his, stopping him in his tracks. She stared up at him, eyes wide with confusion.

"I'm going to fuck you, right here on this cloud."

Her mouth dropped open. Her hands fell from his. He continued unbuttoning her blouse. It fluttered down between them. He tugged her into his arms, his mouth connecting with hers. Her hands rested on his shoulders.

"Why is it such a turn on to hear you say things like that to me?"

He pulled away, grinning.

"I think you're wearing far too much still."

It was taking too long, undressing her as a human would. Impatience flared inside him. He clicked his fingers and in an instant, he'd divested both of them of their clothes. She moved to cover herself, but he took her hands, kissing her fingertips.

"I... What did you do?"

Instead of responding, he pressed her downwards, covering her body with his own. He kissed her again, devouring her mouth. She moaned, her hands clutching his back. She was so soft, pliant under his fingers. He could feel her desire for him pulsating in her veins. He wanted to take his time with her, but his need to feel her was driving him to distraction.

"I feel like my whole body is singing from his touch. I don't even care why we're doing this here. If we get interrupted again I might actually scream."

He cupped one of her breasts, thumb rubbing over the hardened nub. She arched up against him. His other hand found her sex. She was already wet for him. It made his heart pound faster. This desire he felt was unlike anything else.

"Do you have any idea how desperately I want to bury myself in you?"

"Please, I want you to."

Her tone set his entire body on fire. Waiting was no longer an option. He waved a hand. The cloud curled around her ankles, pulling her legs open for him. It then lashed onto her wrists, holding her in place. She stared up at him, grey eyes wide with desire.

"Is this your idea of punishing me?" she asked, straining against the bonds. "Making it impossible for me to touch you."

"Do you want to touch me?"

"Yes, you know I do. How is this fair?"

He smiled.

"Perhaps if you're good, I'll allow you to go free."

His fingers brushed over her sex again, circling her sensitive core. She groaned, wriggling against his hand.

"Please, stop teasing me. I want you so much."

"I didn't think hearing you beg me to take you would be so... sweet."

"I'll beg you as much as you want if it means you'll give it to me. Please, Az."

Her pleas were too much. He pressed her legs open further, staring down at her naked form. *She is so beautiful. I'm utterly at her mercy and she has no idea.* Leaning over her, he kissed her neck, tongue running down her heated skin.

"Az, please, I can't take much more of this. I feel like I'm going to combust."

He gripped her thighs, pressing into her, feeling her enclose him inch by inch. She cried out, her eyes flying open. Her chest heaving with every breath she took.

"Fuck," he grunted.

She encased him in liquid heat. It was unlike anything he imagined. No other human woman he'd been with felt like her. The way her body moulded to his. She was perfect. He released the hold the cloud had on her. Her hands curled around his back, her face buried in his shoulder. She groaned when he pressed deeper, giving her everything he had to offer.

"Az, you feel like nothing else in this world."

He began a slow, torturous pace. She clutched him tighter, letting out a series of garbled curses. He stopped caring he was doing this in full view of Heaven. All his focus was on the woman beneath him. There was electricity between them were their skin met, their bodies joined. Now he knew what she felt like, a human lifetime with her would never be enough.

He burnt with need. Gripping her hips, he thrust harder, needing to take her to heights she'd never met before. Show her that no one else could give her the pleasure he could. He wanted to brand himself on her skin. He needed her to know what it meant to be his.

"Az... look at me."

He leant back a little, staring down into her grey eyes. They were full of heat, lust. She reached up, running her fingers through the hair at the back of his head. Her expression changed, concern falling over her features.

"I need you to tell me this is what you want, that this feels right."

"You feel right. Everything between us is right. Do you doubt me still?"

"No... Not when you look at me like that. Not when you make me feel things I've never experienced before. This isn't like being with a human."

"No, you're with an angel now, Alice, and I don't intend to let you go."

He captured her mouth to stop her from saying anything further.

You're mine, Alice. My human. Do you hear me? Mine.

"*I hear you... I'm yours.*"

He didn't let up. Giving her more, deeper, harder until she begged him to give her a release. Her nails dug into his back, her thighs tightened around him. She was close to exploding all over him. He could feel the tremors across her skin.

"Let go," he whispered in her ear.

She bucked against him, her body trembling, her sex clenching, tightening. She cried out his name as it drove through her. He couldn't hold back against the tidal wave of her climax. He grunted, feeling his own end pulsate through him at an alarming pace.

Alice had once said in her head she wanted to be the balm to his suffering. She was that and so much more. Ever since he'd kissed her the first time, he'd felt calmer. At peace almost. Now, after they had taken the final, irreversible step with each other, he felt a completeness he'd never experienced before. He wasn't quite sure what all these alien feelings were, but he knew he couldn't let her go.

"Az," she whispered, coming down from her high. "You're like ecstasy, except this isn't like any drug I've ever heard of."

He grinned, stroking her hair from her face. She'd worn contacts this evening, but he still thought she was beautiful when she was in her glasses.

"I'm a drug to you?"

"No, you're so much more, but I don't have any words to describe it."

Her heart thundered next to his where they were pressed against each other.

"*If I'm yours... does that make you mine?*"

He took her hands, pinning them next to her head.

"Hmm... is that what you want?"

"Yes."

He smiled. Sometimes she could be quite direct, at others, timid and shy.

"If that's what will make you happy. I have no patience for anyone but you."

She entwined their fingers together, turning her face so she could kiss his hand.

"Being with you makes me happy."

That's all I want. Her happiness.

"Do you want to go home?"

She nodded, kissing his fingers again. He shifted off her, releasing her hands. The next moment, they were dressed. He picked her up, holding her close. He looked up.

Whatever you sent me here for, Father, I don't care anymore. All that matters is her.

His wings appeared and they descended back to Earth together. He fully intended to keep the beautiful girl in his arms safe.

Alice stretched a little when she awoke. Her body still thrummed from Az's touch the night before. *Sex with him... I have no words. It was everything and so much more.*

She pulled the covers off her face, turning to find the angel next to her. His eyes were closed. His long eyelashes stark against his pale skin. She reached up, brushing the lock of auburn hair, which had fallen across his brow, away. He caught her hand before she could retract it, bringing it to his lips. He kissed her fingertips one by one.

"Were you sleeping?" she asked.

"For a time, yes."

She shuffled towards him, pressing her lips to his. He pulled her closer, murmuring his approval against her mouth. It was bliss. Waking up with him and knowing she could be close to Az. Kiss him. Touch him. Whatever reservations she had about wanting an immortal being had well and truly gone out the window. *He's mine.* It felt right.

"Mmm, I want you again, but first, I'm going to make sure you're adequately fed," he said.

"Is that so you can have me several times over?"

"If we didn't have company soon, I would keep you in this bed all day."

She didn't have a response. Heat flooded her cheeks. She was aware of their mutual attraction, but his appetite for her was unexpected. Everything about this was unexpected.

When he'd brought her back to the penthouse, he'd pushed her on the bed and taken her again. Slow and sensual, unlike the intense pounding he'd given her up in the skies.

Still can't believe we had sex on a cloud. When he had me at his mercy... Holy crap that was hot. I wonder if he'll do it again... keeping me restrained whilst he has his way with me.

He slipped from the bed, kissing her forehead. She watched him leave, her mouth growing dry at the sight of him shirtless. She would never tire of seeing him in all his glory. She stretched out, feeling contentment settle in her bones. Grabbing her phone off the bedside table, she knew she'd be in trouble with Chris for not getting in contact with him.

I'm sorry. I should've texted you. I just got distracted.

A minute later, his response appeared.

In a good way I hope?

The best. All I can say is cloud sex.

What?! He fucked you on a cloud?

Yes :) mental isn't it?

I hope it was good.

Good? Chris, he was fucking incredible.

She smiled. It really had been incredible. She put her phone back down on the bedside table. Even though he was making her breakfast in bed, she wanted to hold him again. Her angel.

There was no warning when something exploded out of her. All she saw was black smoke writhing, twisting around her body. She tried to scream, but her mouth stayed firmly shut. Images assaulted her senses. Her eyes rolled back in her head. Visions of the world burning. Buildings crashing down. The land scorched with flame. Ash clouds coating the skies. The dust settling on the blackened earth. And the only person left was her, bathed in smoke. Her hair wild. Her eyes black.

"I am coming," said a voice in her head. "I am coming."

The smoke drove into her mouth, filling her with darkness. She felt it deep in her skin, her bones. When she opened her eyes again, they were pools of black. She launched herself out of the bed before taking shaky steps towards the living room. She needed Azrael. Whatever this was had a message for him.

He turned in the kitchen at the sound of her footfall on the carpet. His eyes widened. He'd dressed in a plain white shirt and chinos, his feet bare.

A voice that sounded nothing like her own erupted from her mouth.

"I am coming."

"Alice?" he whispered, taking a step towards her.

The doors to the elevator dinged. She didn't turn to see who it was when they slid open.

"I am coming to consume you. Heaven. Earth. Hell. The Darkness has awoken. The lands will bleed. Feed my wrath. You have awoken me, Azrael. I will not be contained again. I am coming. I am coming for you all."

Her legs gave out. She collapsed on the carpet, her mouth wide as the smoke billowed out and evaporated into thin air. A sob tore from her throat.

"Az."

He was in front of her in moments, kneeling and pulling her into his arms.

"Shh, shh, it's okay. You're okay."

"What was that?" she sobbed.

He stroked her hair, tensing at her question.

"Lucifer warned me what you might be. I didn't want to listen to him. I didn't want you to be a part of this mess, but you are and I'm sorry. I'm so sorry. Alice, I'm sorry."

There was a cough from their right. Both of them turned at the noise. Standing by the elevator doors, staring at the two of them were a man and a woman. He had dark hair and dark eyes. The woman beside him had long chestnut brown hair and blue eyes. They both looked shocked and confused.

"You must be Ella and Lukas," Azrael said.

Chapter Twelve

The silence between the four of them went on far longer than Alice was comfortable with. She trembled in Azrael's arms, feeling the weight of what just happened crashing down on her. Azrael shifted, picking her up and standing with her in his arms.

"I will explain everything, but I need to deal with what just happened right now. I hope you understand. Please make yourselves comfortable," he said, indicating the sofas with his head.

The girl nodded slowly, reaching out and grasping the man's hand. Azrael strode into the bedroom with her, settling her down on the bed. He knelt before her, taking her hands in his.

"What is the Darkness?" she whispered.

"My Father's wrath."

"What do you mean?"

"It is a long story and one I will tell you, but not now. You need to listen to me very carefully. I think you are its vessel."

"What?"

"The vessel for the Darkness."

Her mind whirled with questions. How could she be a vessel? How could the Darkness take her? Why would God choose her for this? It made no sense. She'd never felt anything like that inside her before.

"That's... I don't understand."

"The Darkness, Lucifer and I, we're all connected. He created it to end everything."

"Why would God want to destroy everything he created?"

He sighed, releasing one of her hands so he could run it through his hair. "I don't know the answer to that."

"Do you think this is why I see you? Because I'm the Darkness."

"You are not the Darkness. The Darkness is a separate entity. You are still linked to us because you are its vessel."

How could she be linked to Azrael, Lucifer and the Darkness? She was a plain girl. Nothing special. And yet she wasn't. She could see angels.

"It said you woke it... Is that because we slept together?"

"Perhaps... or maybe it was because I antagonised my Father."

She raised an eyebrow.

Did you take me up to that cloud and have sex with me in full view of Heaven to piss him off?

"Yes and no."

She folded her arms across her chest. Did he think that was going to fly with her? How could he think that was okay? She wasn't a pawn for him to use as he pleased.

"Well, that just makes me feel a little used."

His eyes flashed with concern.

"Alice, that was not my intention."

He better have a damn good excuse for why the hell he did it.

"Then what was?"

He was silent for several moments before he looked away, his eyes full of regret.

"I can't take you to Heaven. That is as close as I can get. I wanted it to be..."

"Be what?"

"Special for you."

She stared at him, eyes wide. She hadn't expected that to be his reasoning. Why would he want to take her to Heaven? Did he want her to see where he was from? His home?

"And the fact that it pissed off your dad?"

"I wish it hadn't. I didn't want this to happen."

She reached out, cupping his face. His expression made her heart ache. He seemed so conflicted and yet apologetic all at the same time. How could she stay mad at him? Az might be many things, but he still cared for her.

"Special, huh? Do I really mean that much to you?"

He nodded, turning his face into her palm and placing a kiss on it.

"You see me," he whispered. "After hundreds of years alone, you see me."

Tears welled in her eyes. Despite none of this making sense and all of it being terrifying, Azrael still managed to render her speechless. Her heart threatened to burst from her chest. They saw each other.

"We should really see to our guests," she said.

He reached up, pulling her down towards him. She curled up in his lap.

"We should, but I want to hold you first."

She rested her head on his shoulder and settled a hand on his chest. His heart racing against her fingertips. She affected him. The human he'd kept because she intrigued him and now he desired and cared for her. If someone had told her she'd wind up having an angel want her only a few short weeks ago, she'd have told them they were insane.

You really do care about me.

"Yes."

He buried his face in her hair.

"Even though I'm going to end the world?"

"You're mine, Alice. Mine. The Darkness can't have you."

The possessiveness of his tone made her quite sure Azrael wouldn't let her go without a fight. She wasn't sure either of them could stop the Darkness taking over her. If he was right and she was the vessel, she would have no choice.

"You won't bring the end," he whispered. "That's not your fate."

He clutched her tighter. There were so many things he wasn't telling her. She felt him holding back. She didn't like these secrets, but now wasn't the time to hassle him about it. They still had guests and she needed to process everything he'd told her.

"I should get dressed," she said.

She gently pulled away. He got up, helping her to her feet. He waved a hand. When she looked down, she was in a t-shirt and jeans.

"I'm perfectly capable of doing that myself."

He tugged on her hand.

"I want to take care of you."

She raised an eyebrow but said nothing. If that's what he wanted, she wouldn't object. She followed him back out into the living room. Their guests were sitting together on one of the large sofas, their heads pressed together in low conversation.

"I apologise for the slight interruption," Azrael said.

They looked up, eyes wide. Azrael tugged her over to the kitchen and made her sit at the breakfast bar. Another wave of the hand produced tea and muesli for her.

"Eat, please."

He pressed a kiss to the top of her head before moving away. She stared after him.

"Can I offer you a drink?" he asked their guests.

"Um, sure... Tea?" the girl said.

He sat down and with a flick of his wrist, a teapot along with cups, a little jug of milk, sugar and teaspoons appeared. Their two guests stared at the cups.

"As you may have gathered, I am Azrael and that is Alice."

"Ella and Lukas," the man said.

"You're an Archangel?" Ella asked.

Azrael poured them out two cups of tea, which they took without question.

"Yes. I do not know what you know about me, but it has been centuries since I was in Heaven. Hence why I did not know about what they'd been doing."

"I'm sorry, but what the hell was that about when we came in?" Lukas said, his eyes narrowing.

Alice snagged her bowl from the counter, turning in her seat so she could watch and eat at the same time.

"Do you know of the Darkness?"

"Yes, but we don't know what it is. Ella's mother merely told us it was coming one day and that we were created to stand in defence of humanity."

"Who exactly created you?"

Ella looked at Lukas who nodded.

"Ariel and Beleth created me. They possessed two humans, imbued me with half of Lukas' demon soul and placed an angel soul within me. It was only through my declaration of love that my angel soul split in half and was given to Lukas. You see, we share half of each other's souls."

Azrael looked haunted for a moment. Alice wondered if he knew who they were referring to. What they'd said about how they were created was a little insane. She didn't think angels and demons worked together.

"Ariel... I see."

"You knew her?"

"I did."

Alice could see the light surrounding him dimming just a little. Who was this angel to him? She was sure Ariel must be an angel.

"Will you explain to us why there was black smoke coming out of your... companion?" Lukas asked.

"The Darkness is here. My father created it to end Heaven, Hell and Earth. Alice delivered its message to me. Lucifer and I have waited for this day to come since our exile from Heaven."

"Lucifer, as in the Devil?" Ella asked.

"Yes."

The two of them looked stumped for a moment. Alice put her bowl back on the counter, having finished, and took her mug with her. She sat next to Azrael. His hand curled around her waist. Heat radiated from his skin. She tried not to squirm. Thoughts of what they'd done up in the clouds threatened to surface. Thinking about it wouldn't do when they had guests and this whole situation with the Darkness made everything so much more complicated.

"Can I ask why you wanted to meet us?" Lukas said.

"You were created to fight the Darkness. I wish to stop it from destroying everything."

"Then you want our help?"

"In a sense."

Alice knew how much he hated asking anyone for anything. It would grate on her angel.

Ella turned to Lukas.

"It's what we were born to do. We were always going to need allies."

"I know, sweetheart."

Alice leant towards Azrael. She was worried about what they might do if they discovered she was the Darkness' vessel. She hadn't told him about the visions either. She knew now what she'd seen. The end. The scorched plains of Heaven, Earth and Hell.

"You are going to show me what you saw later, Alice. Don't think you can keep such things from me."

She turned to Azrael, startled by his sudden intrusion into her mind.

"Don't do that," she hissed. "Do you even understand the concept of privacy?"

"There is no privacy between you and I."

"Well, there should be."

"Do you want me to punish you again? Because I will not hesitate to tease you until you beg me to stop."

Her face grew hot. She pressed hands to her cheeks, trying to stop the rising tide of her blush. Why did he have to say things like that? He knew exactly what it did to her.

That's not fair.

"I do not play fair, or did you forget?"

She turned away, realising two sets of eyes were on them. Ella's brow furrowed. Lukas looked as though he was suddenly realising that there was more to Alice's relationship with the angel then meets the eye. She wanted the ground to swallow her up. What would they even think about her being with him?

"I have a question," Ella said. "You understandably have a white aura. Why is Alice's black?"

"You see auras?" Azrael asked.

"Yes, it's something I've been able to do since I was a child, long before my full powers manifested. Humans don't have auras, but she does."

Alice tried not to flinch. How could they keep the fact that she was the vessel for the Darkness from the two of them?

"I can only offer you a theory. Alice is the Darkness' messenger."

"Its messenger?"

"Yes. As you saw, it doesn't have a solid form."

Ella and Lukas looked sceptical but didn't comment further. Alice didn't want them to put two and two together.

"I am not asking you to make a decision now. Merely warning you to be ready when the time comes," Azrael said when the silence went on for too long.

"Okay, well, we should really be off," Lukas said. "We'll be in touch."

Azrael nodded. He put a hand to his head, his expression becoming pained. He cursed under his breath. Alice put a hand on his arm.

"What's wrong?"

"He is calling."

"Who?"

"My Father."

She stared at him. *Why is God calling him now?* He stood up and her arm fell. It clearly hurt him to have his father calling. She wanted to soothe away his pain, be there for him always.

"I need to go. I cannot answer him here in your presence."

"What, why?"

"This is a conversation I should have alone if he wants to speak to me."

He began walking away towards the lift. There were so many questions she had, but the most pressing couldn't wait. Alice stood, almost tripping over the coffee table as she ran after him.

"Az," she whispered, catching his arm. "What... What if He wants you to return home? What if He takes you away from me?"

He turned, his expression softening. He reached up, cupping her cheek.

"I have not fulfilled my purpose on Earth. No one is going to take me away from you. I am yours and you are mine. Do not forget that."

He looked over her head at their two guests for a moment before he tugged her towards him. He tipped her face up with one hand.

"I'll always come back to you," he said, his voice low.

Her heart was in her mouth. She wasn't quite sure if this was his way of reassuring her or if he really felt that strongly about the two of them. He leant down, his mouth brushing over hers. Her lips tingled.

"I trust you," she whispered.

He pressed his mouth firmly on hers. She was a little embarrassed about him kissing her in front of Ella and Lukas, but his lips felt like nothing else. The world disappeared for the few moments they were locked together. His tongue swept into her mouth. Az wasn't holding back one bit as he took his fill of her.

Will it ever not feel incredible to be kissed by him?

When he pulled away, she was breathless. He kissed her forehead before releasing her. He put a hand to his head again.

"Go," she said. "I don't like seeing you in pain."

His lip quirked up at the side. He brushed her jaw one last time before he strode away to the lift. Their eyes met when he turned. There was a promise of what was to come when he returned.

I didn't realise just how much he wants me. Damn, my face is on fire.

The doors closed, sealing him away from her. Her heart wrenched painfully.

She turned back to their guests. They both looked a little shell-shocked.

"Um... feel free to finish your drinks," she said, walking back over towards the sofa.

"You and him are... a thing?" Ella asked.

Alice sat down, fidgeting with her hands. She didn't like this business of God calling Azrael. It made her nervous. She wanted to be with her angel. Being separated from him for even a moment felt like an eternity.

It's all so soon, but I feel as though we're meant to be together.

"Um, you could say that."

"I've heard of angels and humans before, but isn't he like an Archangel?"

"He is."

Ella eyed her for a moment before responding.

"Can I ask you what it's like? I know we're half angel, but we're also still technically human so it's not the same."

Alice didn't think her face could get any redder.

"Sweetheart, is that really appropriate?" Lukas asked, staring at her with wide eyes.

"It's okay," Alice said. "It's not like being with a human or anything. He's intense on every single level."

Lukas shook his head, putting his hand on his girlfriend's arm. She looked at Alice with a knowing smile.

"Well, we'll be off then," Lukas said. "It was nice to meet you. Ella has your number."

Alice nodded at the two of them as they stood. She didn't watch them walk away. After Ella's questions, she wasn't quite sure what to make of the two of them.

A few minutes later, the doors of the lift dinged and then she was alone. All her thoughts centred on her angel again.

What does God want with my Az?

Chapter Thirteen

Azrael landed on the roof of his building. The wind fluttered his wings. He stared up at the sky. Heaven was beyond. He could feel its presence looming over him. He could no longer feel the pull of his father. He waited, not knowing what his father wanted. After all these centuries, it would be strange to hear his voice again.

"I'm here," he said. "What is it you want with me, Father?"

There was a deafening silence. He'd blocked out all the permeating noises of human society. It was him and the wind softly brushing against his skin. Clouds were gathering above him. A storm was brewing. He could feel it in the air.

"Is this some kind of joke to you? Why would you call me when you have no intention of speaking to me?"

Typical. Is he trying to lure me away from Alice?

He sat down on the edge of the roof, his legs dangling off the side. His wings folded against his back. Alice was safe in the penthouse. He had nothing to worry about on that score. The floor he occupied of the building was warded against anything or anyone who might wish to take her. He didn't look over when he felt a presence by his side. He could see their legs dangling over the side of the building next to his.

"It has been a long time," said a feminine voice.

He ran a hand through his hair. This was the very last person he wished to speak to.

Centuries and I still despise her.

"You have been busy in my absence," he replied.

"Azrael, you know I am sorry for what happened."

"As if such things matter now. You called me using His voice, did you not?"

"I apologise for the deception. I could not be sure you would answer otherwise."

She was right. He would never have answered a call from her. Resentment built in his chest. She'd betrayed him the day she stood with their father. After everything they'd been through together. He clamped down on the memories. Now was not the time for bringing up old wounds.

"What do you want, Ariel?"

"Why have you sought out my daughter?"

"I did not know she was your creation until she told me."

He was not about to reveal he'd known about her because he'd spoken to Lucifer. His brother hated Ariel more than he did.

"That did not answer my question."

"If you care so much about what I wanted her for, then you should ask her yourself. I owe you no explanations."

He got to his feet, stalking away towards the door to the roof. He was done with this conversation already. He wanted to get back to Alice.

"Azrael..."

He stopped, turning back to Ariel, eyes blazing with unconcealed fury.

"What is it? Do you want to run off to Daddy again and report on my actions? Is that what this is?"

She flinched.

"I had no choice."

"There is always a choice. Don't test me. You know who will win if you try."

Ariel was merely a guardian angel. She was no match for him. He had the might of an Archangel.

"Please, you do not know how sorry I am for it all."

"Sorry isn't good enough. You knew what we were trying to achieve. You agreed with us and yet when the time came, you were the coward who told Him of our decision to stand against Him. Where was your loyalty?"

Ariel stood, taking a step towards him, her hand out.

"There hasn't been a day when I haven't thought of you."

He clenched his fists. Her thinking of him meant nothing at all. She'd been his closest confidant, but nothing stings quite like betrayal. Tamping down on his frustration. His pain. He stared at her for what seemed like an eternity. He could see the resemblance she had to Ella. Yet her half angel, half demon, human child was more than Ariel would ever be. He could feel it.

"You should not waste your thoughts on me. I have everything I ever need here."

He might not have had it before, but now, now he had Alice. She was everything he never knew he needed. Their connection with each other surpassed reason or explanation. They belonged to each other.

"You don't wish to return home?"

Her brow furrowed.

"You know very well that is impossible. I have not fulfilled my purpose. Even if I was allowed to return, do you think I would wish to be subjected to the scorn of our brothers and sisters? I have lived on Earth too long."

Ariel looked conflicted, sad almost. She dropped her hand, her head bowing.

"I wish it had never come to this."

Nothing she said would change things. She'd made her choice and they'd all suffered the consequences of their father's wrath.

"You brought this upon yourself. Good day, sister," he spat.

He strode away, wrenching open the door to the building. It slammed shut behind him. His heart pounded in his chest, wrenching painfully.

When Ella had mentioned her mother was Ariel, earlier, it had taken everything he had not to react to the name. He didn't wish to think about his sister let alone see her again. She betrayed them. She was responsible. Nothing would ever change those facts.

He took the stairs two by two. There was only one thing he wanted at that moment and nothing was going to stand in his way.

Alice paced the living room. He was taking far too long. The morning had been full of surprises. None of them pleasant. Being separated from him made her anxious. Az was the most important person in her life. She wasn't quite sure when that had occurred, but she didn't care. She would go to the ends of the earth for him.

Wringing her hands, she stopped by the huge window, staring out over the London skyline. *Where had he gone?* This wasn't helping matters. She needed a distraction. She put her hand on the glass. Her phone buzzed in her pocket. She tugged it out. It was Chris. She hadn't replied to him earlier after the crap with the Darkness.

"Hi."

"Ally, love, you left me hanging again."

"I'm sorry, Chris. Something happened and... and now I'm really worried about Az."

"What is it?"

"He had to go because he got a call from someone and I'm worried he'll have to go back. I can't deal with it if he's taken away from me."

"Slow down, what do you mean? You're not making sense."

"I need him, Chris. Like air. I know I haven't talked about this properly to you... explained our feelings for each other. It's hard to know where to start."

The sound of the lift dinging startled her. She turned, finding Azrael striding towards her, his face a picture of determination.

"Az...?"

"Alice? Is that him?" Chris said.

"I have to go."

She hung up. Az barely gave her a chance to look up at him. His mouth crashed down on hers, his hands winding around her back. The phone fell from her hand. He pinned her to the window, devouring her lips before his tongue pressed against them, demanding entry. She relented, his presence overloading her senses.

His fingers found their way under her t-shirt, tracing lines across her skin. She arched into him, her body flaming with need immediately. She was aware in the back of her mind she should ask him where he'd been and what his father had wanted, but his mouth against hers was far too intoxicating.

He tugged her t-shirt over her head, followed by her bra. His mouth latched onto her nipple, tongue running circles around it. She groaned, her fingers tangling in his hair when he bit down. His other hand was busy with the button of her jeans before he tugged the zip down.

"Off, now," he growled.

"Az... what's the rush?" she asked, breathlessly.

He didn't reply, tugging her jeans down, taking her underwear with them. He was on his knees in front of her, kissing her stomach. She trembled, not knowing quite what all this attention was about. She shouldn't be complaining, but there was a nagging voice in her head. Telling her something was wrong.

He pressed her legs open and he buried his face in her sex. She lost all coherent thought. His tongue lashed against her, sending tremors up her spine. She pressed a hand to the window, steadying herself. The other buried in his auburn hair, tugging at the strands.

"Fuck, fuck, Az!"

She couldn't help but cry out his name over and over. He held her in place when she bucked against him. Her vision blurred at the edges. The intensity of his tongue set her whole world alight. He was relentless, but not quite allowing her to fall over the edge. He had her wound up so tight, she could hardly breathe.

"Please, I can't take it... please."

There was no relief. He seemed hell-bent on driving her higher than she'd ever been before.

Please, I'm begging you. It's too much.

It was almost as if he was playing her body like a musical instrument. She burnt everywhere, her skin tingling. Her fingers dug into his hair, trying to pry him away. He took her hand and pinned it to the window.

It started with tremors running down her back, followed by tiny sparks dancing across her skin. She panted, utterly surrendering herself to him. Her eyes rolled back in her head. She could've sworn she saw stars in her vision. It all exploded at once. She cried out, her legs almost buckling under the intensity. He held her up, pulling away to look up at her. His green eyes blazed with unending desire.

It was a long while before she stopped trembling. He got to his feet when she sagged against the window. He gripped her shoulders, turning her around. He ran his fingers down her spine. She wasn't sure she could take any more. He nudged her legs open, his hands running over her behind. He tugged her towards him before forcing her to bend over slightly, her palms flat against the window. She felt him pressing against her entrance.

She turned her head to look at him. He'd done his angel thing and undressed within the blink of an eye. Her mouth dried up. The sight of him always did things to her. He pressed into her, forcing her to take it all at once. She yelped. He leant over her, his breath hot against her ear.

"You're mine, Alice. I'm going to fuck you against this window until you lose yourself to me all over again. Nothing is going to keep us apart. Do you understand?"

"Yes," she whispered.

She trembled when he began a punishing pace. Whatever happened when he'd left had clearly rattled him. She could tell that much from his actions. He wanted to lose himself in her. It made her heart ache for him. She wanted to ask questions, but she could barely form a sentence. His fingers dug into her hip, the other hand curling around her stomach, holding her to him.

"She's everything to me."

She wasn't sure he'd meant to send that thought to her.

"I don't want to think about my sister anymore. I just want this, here, right now. Sweet Alice, I need her. Only her. She is mine and I am hers. We belong to each other."

Thoughts raced through her mind at a hundred miles an hour. His sister? He'd said God had called him. Had he seen another angel? And he thought they belonged to each other. Her heart lurched. Those were his private thoughts, not ones he'd allowed her to hear.

He grunted, pressing deeper inside her. He kissed her neck and shoulder. She had to put aside all the burning questions. She focused on the sensations he elicited. She wanted to be in this moment with him. For him.

We belong together. That's all that matters right now. The rest can wait.

He held her tighter, his fingers curling around her throat. She tried not to flinch. He wouldn't hurt her, but it didn't make it any less disconcerting how much he had her at his mercy.

"Let go, Alice, I want to feel you," he whispered in her ear.

His commanding tone was met with a cry from her. Her body shook. Her second climax racing through her. His hand tightened around her neck. His breath fanned across her cheek.

"I'm not done with you yet."

Can you at least make this a little more comfortable if you're going to insist on taking me yet again?

He tugged her up, flush against his chest. His thumb ran across her bottom lip. She was slick with sweat, but his skin was cool against hers. He spun her around. His eyes were dark with lust. She quaked under the intensity of his gaze. He backed her towards the sofa, forcing her down onto the L shape, her legs dangling off the side. He knelt before her and pressed into her again.

He was the most perfect being imaginable. The way they fit together. How he felt when he filled her. They were made for each other. A human and an Archangel. Yet, she knew she wasn't just human. She was a vessel and one day, that would threaten to tear them apart. She felt it deep in her bones. The sticky feeling of the Darkness hadn't left her completely.

She sat up, clutching Az as he thrust inside her. She held him to him for all she was worth. Tears ran down her cheeks, falling on his shoulder. He didn't stop, but he tucked his fingers under her chin, forcing her to look at him.

"Why are you crying?"

Chapter Fourteen

nstead of answering, she pressed her mouth to his, kissing him despite the unabated tears streaming down her face.

I'm afraid.

His hands tangled in her hair.

"Of what?"

Of everything the Darkness showed me. Of everything destined to come to pass. Of losing you.

He pulled away, staring down at her with emotions she didn't understand. He wiped her tears from her cheeks. Her fears were all too real to her. The one that mattered the most was in front of her. If she lost him, she would lose herself entirely. He anchored her to the world. The Darkness would consume her without Azrael.

"I'm yours," he whispered. "Do you understand what that means to have an Archangel at your feet? I will lay down my immortal life for you."

"What? You can't die for me."

He smiled, brushing her cheek with his thumb.

"You're right. I can't die. But I will protect you at all costs."

"You're going to make me cry again."

She wrapped her legs around him, pressing him closer, deeper inside her.

"We can't have that."

She felt a wave of happiness flood through her. It broke through her fears, filling her with a sense of peace. She raised an eyebrow at him.

"Are you doing that?"

He grinned wickedly.

"Perhaps."

"I'd much rather you use that on my body."

He ran his fingers down her back. It sent sparks across her skin. She arched into his touch, revelling in the feelings he elicited.

"Don't stop," she whispered.

He continued stroking her skin. She felt the warmth of his power washing over her. He leant down, kissing her shoulder and neck. Her fingers dug into the hard muscle of his back. She never wanted this moment to end, but there was something else she wanted to ask him.

"Az..."

"Mmm?"

She drew her fingers down his back. He looked at her, his eyes narrowing.

"Would you perhaps consider, you know, doing it with them out?"

"Are you asking me to get my wings out for you?"

She bit her lip, nodding. She had no idea how he was going to react to her request. She wanted the full force of his angelic nature on show because it was who Az really was.

He tucked his hands under her behind before he stood. Nothing in his expression gave away what he thought. He carried her into the bedroom before setting her down on the bed. He stood at the end, staring down at her. Her gaze ran down his chest and lower.

Fuck me, he is too beautiful for words. I still don't understand what he sees in me, but I know we are each other's.

"Is this what you want?" he asked.

The air behind him shimmered. A soft halo of light appeared above his head. His brilliant white wings flared outwards, taking up half the room with their size. She swallowed, hard, sitting up on her elbows. She had no words. She put a hand up, curling her finger and beckoning him over. His lips quirked up.

I most definitely want you to come here.

He crawled over her, stealing her lips in a searing kiss. She lay back, staring up at her angel with unabashed admiration. She reached up, running her fingers through the feathers gently. He hissed slightly.

"Alice, that tickles," he complained.

"Do you want me to stop?"

He shuddered, shaking his head.

"No... No, don't. I crave your touch."

Her eyes widened slightly at his admission. Her fingers brushed over the underside of his wing again. He closed his eyes, taking a breath. She wanted to make him feel good, just like he always did for her. She cupped his face, running a thumb over his bottom lip.

"Lie down, please."

He opened his eyes, frowning for a moment. She shifted out from under him and pressed him down on the bed. His wings splayed out over the covers. She almost faltered at the sight of him. She straddled him, careful not to kneel on the feathers. He gripped her thighs when she sunk down on him. She leant over, trailing her fingers over his feathers. He groaned, closing his eyes, his fingers tightening around her.

My beautiful angel. I don't know if I can describe my feelings for you. I just know I want you forever.

"You have me forever. I'm eternally yours," he murmured.

She captured his mouth, pouring all of her feelings into the kiss. She wanted him to know the depth of her affections. To know that what she felt for him was beyond mortal words. He wrapped his wings around them, encasing the two of them in their own little world. It was at that moment she knew what her feelings for him truly were.

She loved Azrael.

There was no question.

She was in love with the Archangel of Death.

And she wanted to cry all over again, knowing her heart was going to be torn in half the moment the Darkness took her away from him.

He left her sleeping. Her hair was mussed, sticking up in places where he'd tugged on it earlier. His heart stopped momentarily. She was the most beautiful being in this world.

They'd spent the rest of the day in bed together, enjoying each other's bodies in every which way they could. He would never get enough of her. Alice was the balm to everything. She gave him a reason to live again.

Before she'd dropped off to sleep, she'd shown him the visions she'd had when the Darkness had inhabited her body. He knew what would come to pass if he didn't do something about it. And he would do anything to keep her safe.

He turned to the window. The storm outside raged, the rain battering down on the glass. Lightning streaked across the sky followed shortly by the crack of thunder. The storm signalled the arrival of the Darkness on Earth. He walked towards it, his wings spread out behind his back. He was glad Alice was asleep. He wasn't quite sure she would forgive him if she saw him step through the glass into the nothingness beyond it.

The rain battered down on his bare chest, his wings becoming thoroughly soaked within moments. He beat them, flying upwards until he landed on the roof. He stared up at the dark skies. He didn't feel the cold nor the rain against his skin.

"Is this what you wanted, Father? Did you wish to bring ruin to everything you built?" he shouted. "Did you want to watch us all suffer?"

Anger and frustration rushed through him. His punishment for disobedience was severe, but ending the world was something else.

"This has to be your idea of a joke. Why her? Why did you have to make her the vessel? Why are we connected? Is this what you meant? Is this how I bring the end?"

He paced away, unable to keep still. His whole body radiated with tension, distress. All of his emotions bubbled up to the surface, threatening to burst through the dam.

"Tell me one thing... Just one damn thing! What is the purpose of making me feel human emotions? Do you think I want to feel these things about her? Do you? Do you think I want to... to... to love her?"

He sunk to his knees, feeling the weight of his words crash over him. He loved the girl destined to destroy Heaven, Earth and Hell. The girl his father had chosen to be the vessel for the Darkness. The girl who could see him for who he really was. A broken angel. He wasn't quite sure when it had happened or how, but it was true.

He loved Alice.

"Is it really what you wanted for me? I don't understand why this would be your plan. I don't think I have ever understood any of your motives."

He wished his father was there and really listening to him. It had been so long since he'd heard the voice of the Divine. Yet, Alice had filled the unending void inside him. Her presence at his side was all he needed. He would find a way for her to remain there, permanently.

"Does it even matter what you planned? I don't know that it does. All I'm sure of is she matters. I won't let her be destroyed by the Darkness even if I have to give up everything. She is mine and I am hers. We belong to each other. You stranded me here, but I no longer want to return home."

He got to his feet, staring up at the skies again. God didn't care. He was content to let his sons rot.

"You hear me, Father! I refuse to return to your side. I don't belong to you any longer. I belong to her. Only her. You cannot command me any longer. I'm going to stop you from destroying everything if it's the last thing I do."

The next moment, something slammed into him, sending him careening to the floor. Hands pinned him to the ground. He stared up into the dark features of his brother.

"Shouting at dear old Dad isn't going to get you anywhere, brother," Lucifer said.

"Fuck you."

He threw Lucifer off him and got to his feet. His brother stood, dusting himself off. He was thoroughly drenched, his immaculate black suit dripping.

"That's no way to greet your sibling."

"And crashing into me is?"

What the hell is he doing here? Did he hear what I said to Father?

"Tsk, Azrael, if you had been paying attention, you would've heard me coming."

He growled, low. He was in no mood for Lucifer's theatrics. The moment of privacy was gone, rudely interrupted.

"What do you want now?"

"It's here, is it not?"

"Yes."

There was no point in denying it. Lucifer was going to find out the Darkness had awoken regardless.

"And you know what she is now, don't you?"

"Yes."

"And you still won't give her to me."

He clenched his fists. Lucifer was never getting his hands on Alice as long as he was around to protect her.

"It would serve no purpose. The Darkness won't allow you to kill its vessel. You should be focusing your energies on stopping it, not murdering an innocent girl."

"Innocent? I hardly call the Darkness' vessel, innocent. Though, I do wonder why you are so protective of one small, human girl."

He tried to reign in his temper, but Lucifer's grin made him want to curl his hands around his brother's throat. It wouldn't do Alice any favours if his brother found out what was between them. If anything, it would make the situation worse.

"She is innocent. She didn't ask for this. He is the one we should be blaming."

Alice had the misfortune of God deciding she would burn the world. Even if he didn't care for her, it was still a miserable fate for anyone to suffer.

"If you hadn't insisted on involving our trusted sister, then none of us would be in this mess."

"That is on Ariel. She came to see me today after I discovered her little daughter and her boyfriend. You knew, didn't you?"

"That she was involved in their creation? Of course, I knew. Nothing happens in Hell without my knowledge. How is our sister?"

He didn't particularly want to talk about Ariel.

"Apologetic, yet her supposed remorse was disingenuous."

Lucifer was silent for a long moment. His wings curled up against his back. He looked up at the skies.

"Why were you shouting at Father? Do you think He'd really be listening to you?"

"Does it matter?"

"I do wonder at you. I thought you wished to return home and yet, here I find you telling Him you refuse to return to His side. Tell me, Azrael, who is it you belong to now?"

He flew at his brother, his fist connecting with Lucifer's jaw. He was too riled up to care any longer. Fed up with his father. Fed up with Lucifer and his questions. He was done with all of it. Lucifer's head snapped back. There was a red mark on his perfect skin. He growled, launching himself at Azrael. Fists flew between them, each landing several punches on each other.

"What is this, brother? Can't you admit you've fallen under the spell of a human?" Lucifer said.

"Fuck you."

He flew upwards, wings beating before he shot downwards. He slammed Lucifer into the floor, a dent forming in the concrete. His brother laughed.

"Oh dear, I think I've hit too close to home."

Lucifer threw Azrael off him before pinning him to the floor with his foot. Azrael strained underneath his brother. He didn't want to hurt him.

"Oh, well, this is rich. She's made you weak, brother. I did wonder why you wouldn't give her to me in the first place. Could it be you feel things for the girl who is meant to end the world?"

Azrael didn't have time to respond. The door to the roof flew open and out walked Alice. Her eyes were pools of black. Smoke trailed from her fingertips. The rain plastered her hair to her face within minutes, but she didn't seem to notice. She pointed to Azrael.

"He is mine."

Chapter Fifteen

*A*lice took measured steps towards the two angels. Azrael struggled under Lucifer's foot, desperate to go to her. The Darkness had consumed her again. He needed to stop this. He could chuck his brother off, but he'd much rather Lucifer released him of his own accord.

"Get off me," he hissed.

Lucifer was too busy staring at the approaching woman to hear him.

"He is mine, Morningstar. You will release him to me," she said.

"You think I take orders from you?" Lucifer replied.

Smoke shot out from her fingers, curling around Lucifer's wrists, pinning him in place.

"I am His wrath. You will cower when I come for you."

She reached them, her hand curling around Lucifer's neck. She picked him up, launching him off the side of the building. Azrael stared up at her with confusion.

How is it possible for her to throw Lucifer around like he's a ragdoll?

"Alice?"

She knelt down, cupping his face.

"You have bound yourself to my vessel. She cares for you, angel. You will be with me until the end."

"I have no interest in being a part of your destruction."

He sat up, pushing her hand away. Alice could touch him but not the Darkness in her form.

"Return her to me."

Alice blinked, her black eyes unnerving.

"Azrael, this is why I told you to let me have her before this started," Lucifer said.

He landed on the roof again, his expression a picture of irritation. Alice stood, smoke curling around her feet. It rose, circling around her back until a pair of huge, dark wings appeared.

"You will not stand in my way, Morningstar. I will end you."

"Lucifer, get out of here before you antagonise it further," Azrael said.

As much as he hated Lucifer at that moment, he didn't wish him dead. His brother looked between him and Alice. He shook his head, taking to the skies. Alice watched him before turning back to Azrael.

"You wish to have your precious human back? She wants you too. I can feel her trying to push me out. A pity. Her mind is no match for me. One day, I will consume every part of her and you'll have nothing left of the human you adore so much."

Alice fell to her knees, smoke billowing out of her mouth. It took to the skies before it evaporated. She almost toppled over onto her face, but Azrael caught her. He held her close, wrapping his arms around her back. She coughed several times.

"Az," she whimpered.

"Shh, shh, I'm here."

He kissed her hair. His heart ached for her.

"I was asleep. It made me come up here."

"I know."

She shivered. *She must be freezing.* The rain continued to batter down around them. Lightning streaked across the sky. He stood, picking her up and carrying her into the building.

Her skin was cold, clothes plastered to her body. He couldn't leave her like this. Heat washed over the two of them. She blinked rapidly. They were both dry again, but she still felt far too cold.

He took her to the penthouse. He tucked the both of them up in bed, holding her close.

"You're so warm," she whispered, her face pressed into his chest.

"I need you to get warm again."

"I heard what it said to you."

He stiffened slightly.

"It's okay, Az. I'm glad you're safe from him even if it meant being consumed by that thing again."

"I wasn't in danger. I didn't wish to hurt him, not really. Years of anger and frustration boiled over between the two of us."

"Then why did it come after you?"

"Your feelings for me are affecting it."

She pulled away, staring up at him with wide eyes.

I could stare into those slate grey eyes for hours.

"How is that possible?"

"It has seen inside your head. It is bound to your body. I don't think it can help it despite what the Darkness might say."

"Because I care for you, by extension, it does too?"

"It is merely my theory, yes."

"I guess it means it won't harm you then."

He stroked her hair from her face.

"No. I don't think it will. You heard it. It wants me with you until the end."

"I don't want us to be apart."

She reached up, curling her fingers around his neck, tugging him down. She kissed him. It wasn't a sweet kiss. He could feel her desperation, her longing pouring out of her. He held her face, fingers curling into her hair. He'd give her what she needed. It hurt him to see her so affected by the Darkness and its presence.

"Az, make love to me, please," she whispered against his mouth.

The word love almost made him pause. *She doesn't know I love her.* He pressed Alice down on the bed. If she wanted him to make love to her, then that's exactly what he'd do. No further questions asked. But tonight wasn't the right time to reveal his feelings to her. Not after what occurred.

Soon, Alice, soon you'll know how much I burn for you.

Alice hadn't been to work in a week. She hadn't wanted to leave Az's side. Not when the Darkness could overtake her at any time. She was terrified of it wreaking havoc across London if they went out.

She'd finally managed to have a long conversation with Chris about what was really going on. He'd insisted he take time off work to see her but she'd refused. She didn't want her best friend here where he could get hurt. He was safer in Edinburgh where the Darkness couldn't get to him.

Being cooped up in the penthouse wasn't doing Az or Alice any favours. He was withdrawn and broody after what happened with Lucifer and the Darkness. His dark mood only faded when he pinned her down and fucked her until she couldn't take it any longer. She blushed every time she thought of how he'd made a meal out of her over the breakfast bar and a particularly steamy incident in the shower.

Her phone buzzed on the kitchen counter several times. She almost jumped at the noise. Looking down she noted a series of messages from Ella. They hadn't heard from the angel, demon hybrids all week.

We want to help.

Meet us at Fright Night later.

The others will be there too. This affects all of us.

"Az..."

The angel looked up from where he was fiddling with his laptop on the sofa. His beautiful eyebrows drawn down. She went over to him, wanting to soothe away his frown. Taking the laptop out of his hands, she placed it on the coffee table and straddled him.

"To what do I owe this pleasure?" he asked, his eyes sparkling with desire when he looked her up and down.

She gave him her phone. Whilst he looked at it, she ran her fingers down his chest before tucking them under his grey t-shirt. His muscles tensed under her touch. He let out a sharp breath when her fingers brushed lower, finding his belt and unbuckling it.

"You're a very distracting woman," he said.

"And you're a very handsome angel who I want very much to have my hands all over."

He raised an eyebrow, still intent on her phone.

"Is that so?"

She didn't respond. No matter how many times they did this, she always craved more of him. He was addictive. And the fact remained, she loved the angel. Telling him such a thing, however, proved impossible. With the end of the world on the horizon, it should be the perfect time. The threat of the Darkness consuming her held her back. She didn't want to ruin these moments with him with declarations. If she told him, she'd never be able to let him go. She was sure of that much.

She freed him, marvelling at the sight of her beautiful angel, already ready and wanting. She could tell he wasn't prepared for what she did next by the groan of pleasure tearing from his mouth. Shuffling off him, she dropped to her knees on the floor. She hadn't done this since that first night when he'd admitted he desired her. She took him in her mouth, savouring the taste of him against her tongue. His fingers curled into her hair. He wasn't asking her to stop.

"What did I do to deserve your exquisite mouth around me?"

I want to see you smile.

She glanced up at him. His eyes were glittering with wicked mischief. His mouth was curved up at the sides. It was all she needed to see. She concentrated on pleasuring him. He hissed, his fingers digging into her skull when she took him deeper into her mouth.

"We'll go this evening... I guess we... Fuck, Alice... We need to speak to them all.... Fuck. Fuck."

He panted, encouraging her to increase her pace.

"Don't stop," he whispered. "Just don't stop."

Having him plead made her heart hammer in her chest. Her phone dropped from his hand onto the sofa. His other hand dug into her hair, pressing her down further until she couldn't take much more. She pulled back, needing to take several deep breaths.

He leant down, his mouth pressed to her ear, hands on her shoulders.

"Tell me, are you wet for me right now?"

"Yes," she whispered.

"Do you like to have me at your mercy?"

"Yes."

His fingers tightened on her shoulders.

"Does it turn you on to see me so affected by you?"

"Yes."

"Tell me what you want to do to me."

"I want to straddle you, to feel you inside me, to fuck you, to make you come."

He growled low in his throat. One hand curled around her chin, forcing her to turn her head. He kissed her. There was no gentleness to it. Searing heat and passion sparked between them.

He tugged her back up into his lap. She'd worn a dress today, but Az didn't stop to tear her underwear off. Pushing it to the side, she sank down on him. The low groan escaping from his mouth set her body on fire. They ground against each other furiously, lips fused together.

You are my everything. My world. My reason for existing. You and only you.

Az didn't often listen to her thoughts any more. It was only during their most intimate moments when they communicated without words.

"And you are mine. Only mine."

He gripped her hips, increasing their pace. She wanted a release from the tension she felt building inside her. Only he could give her that. He never failed to bring about an earth-shattering ending.

I want to forget for one moment that we're running out of time. I never want these moments with him to end. It breaks me in half when I think of what's to come. I can still feel it inside me. Waiting. Biding its time.

He pulled away, staring up at her with confusion. She almost cursed. He'd heard what she'd thought. She hadn't meant to think those things. Being with him was bittersweet.

"Alice..."

"Don't." She pressed her hand to his mouth. "Don't, Az."

"Alice, it hurts me knowing how much pain the Darkness is causing you. Please don't shut me out."

Tears welled in her eyes. Why did it always come back to the same thing? The Darkness was a curse. It was driving a wedge between them.

"I can't. I can't have this conversation. It's not fair. None of it is fair. It's killing me, Az. It's breaking me to think about the end. You told me you'll protect me, but you can't protect me from this. You can't save me from the Darkness and I think you know that."

They both stilled, staring at each other. Her hand remained over his mouth. She didn't want to hear the words he might say. She wanted to take back what she'd said. He reached up, gently tugging her hand away. His green eyes intent on hers.

"I know."

She didn't think her heart could hurt any more, but the finality of those two words sent a new wave of pain rushing through her. They were on borrowed time. Tears fell down her cheeks. She no longer cared.

"I...I..."

She wanted to say those three words she was keeping locked up inside her, but they refused to come out. Why couldn't she just tell him? Why wasn't it easy?

My feelings, Az. It's too hard for me to express those words.

"Whatever it is you feel for me, Alice, be assured I feel it for you too," he whispered.

Those words broke her more than any others. She buried her face in his shoulder and sobbed. He wrapped his arms around her, holding her close. He stroked her hair, soothing her with his presence, his simple touch.

"I'm sorry my Father did this to you. He is not always the benevolent God humans seem to think He is. I wish I understood why He chose you."

"Why did He exile you from Heaven?" she asked, her voice quiet and unsteady.

"I disobeyed Him in the most fundamental way. I refused to kill for Him any longer despite it being my purpose. He cast me out to force me to accept I would always bring death to the world."

"And Lucifer?"

"Lucifer wanted free will to be given to angels just as He had done for humanity. Several angels agreed with us, but... someone betrayed us to our father. They refused to side with us when He discovered what we wished."

"Was it Ella's mother?"

His arms around her tightened.

"Yes."

"I'm sorry, Az. I can't imagine what it's been like for you. Here I am, crying all over you and you must hate that. I feel stupid. I don't want to cause you further suffering."

She felt a rumble of laughter from his chest.

"Alice, I only suffer when we're apart. You're welcome to expel all your tears on my t-shirt."

"Don't say that just to make me feel better."

She sniffled, trying to stem the tide.

"I'm not. Don't you know all I want is your happiness?"

"Do you?"

He kissed the top of her head.

"It's all that matters to me."

"You're my happiness in case you hadn't realised it yet."

"Are you quite done crying? Because I'd like to finish making love to you."

She pulled away from his shoulder, staring at him with wide eyes. He reached up, wiping her cheeks with his thumb. His eyes sparkled with affection. Her heart thumped at the sight of it.

"What did I do to deserve you?" The words tumbled out against her will.

"I should ask what I did to deserve you, but I don't think we'd come to any satisfactory answers."

He was right. Questioning it was pointless. They'd already established what they meant to each other went beyond words.

"Kiss me."

And he did.

Chapter Sixteen

hey walked into Fright Night together hand in hand. There weren't any patrons in the bar. Ella and Lukas sat in the corner along with Daisy. Standing at the bar was Neave, another man Alice didn't recognise and Gavin. Towards the back was a woman with grey eyes which matched her own, Izzy and a dark-haired man with a scar over his eyebrow. The last two occupants were a girl with red hair sitting in the lap of a man with bright blue eyes.

Alice edged closer to Az, feeling a little out of place. She hadn't realised they'd have gathered so many people together, but the Darkness was a threat to them all. He glanced at her, his green eyes softening.

"It'll be fine. I'm here. I won't let anyone hurt you."

She smiled. She did feel a little safer with him by her side. She was concerned about them discovering what she was. Ella stood, coming over to them. She looked a little tense.

"You came."

"Yes," Az said, his eyebrow raised.

"I suppose introductions are in order. I think you've met Neave, Gavin and Daisy, but that's Jack."

She pointed at the party by the bar.

"Over there is Dalia. She's the Alpha for the werewolf pack and with her is Izzy and Rex and lastly, Alistair and Grace, our resident witches."

Alice half waved, trying to be polite. Az just stared at each of them with an inscrutable expression.

"I do not like this."

Neither do I.

"Just stay close to me."

She wasn't about to leave his side. Az was her only form of protection against anyone who wished to do her harm. Who knew what would happen if they knew she was the Darkness' vessel.

"Who'd have thought we'd be graced with an actual angel?" Alistair said, his blue eyes shining with amusement.

"Shut up," Grace hissed, smacking him on the chest.

"I'm sure he's not offended."

She grabbed his ear, twisting it until he yelped.

"Behave."

He pouted until she released his ear.

"Cruel woman."

"And yet you love me anyway."

Alice tried not to smile. Despite never having met the witches before, she already liked the two of them.

"We asked you to come because we need to talk about the threat of the Darkness," Ella said.

"I assumed as much," Az said.

"Do you want to sit?"

Alice nodded. She found Gavin's eyes on her. They were narrowed to slits. She fidgeted, her hand tightening in Azrael's. He didn't seem to notice. He tugged her away towards the bar, making sure she sat down on one of the stools. He stood next to her, his hand resting on her thigh.

I don't like the way the vampires are looking at me.

Az didn't respond to her comment. He looked around the room, eying each person in turn. He would know what they thought about him if he cared to look in their heads. They all moved closer, crowding around the bar.

"The Darkness is a threat to all of us," Ella said. "As Azrael told us, it has been sent to destroy Heaven, Hell and Earth."

Alice curled her hand around Az's back. She didn't feel remotely safe sitting so close to the two male vampires who were still staring at her. It was unnerving. Az's fingers tightened on her leg.

"The Darkness is his wrath and He is not someone to be taken lightly," Az said.

"You are referring to God, right?" Daisy asked, leaning over the bar to look at the two of them.

Az nodded once.

"As if my life couldn't get any weirder," she mumbled, sitting back down.

"So, let me get this straight," Neave said. "The same God who created all of us has now sent something to destroy everything?"

"Yes," Az replied.

"And why would He have any reason to do such a thing?"

"Why does He have a reason to do anything? He is God. His reasons are his own."

Alice knew that wasn't exactly the truth. It had everything to do with what Lucifer and Azrael had done. Telling them that would only cause more problems.

"Does it perhaps have to do with your exile from Heaven?" Gavin asked, his eyes still intent on Alice.

"My exile from Heaven is not part of this discussion."

"Oh, I think it is. I know the stories about you and Lucifer."

"I don't trust that vampire."

He keeps staring at me. Do you think he knows?

"Look, we're getting off topic here," Ella interjected. "It doesn't matter why or how. What matters is what we're going to do about it."

"And we're meant to trust the angel who awoke the Darkness?" Gavin asked.

"I don't trust you either," Az said.

Alice almost groaned.

Don't start a fight with him. It's not worth it.

"Well, this is off to a flying start," Alistair said, earning a glare from Grace.

The shifters remained silent, staring at the rest of them with interest. Alice had liked Izzy. The man with a scar, who Ella had said was named Rex, had his arm wrapped around her shoulder. *That must be the father of her baby.* She hoped they would all live long enough for Izzy to have her kid. The thought of all these people being snuffed out by the Darkness made her head hurt.

She hopped off the stool, tearing away from Azrael for a moment.

"We didn't come here to argue. We came because we can't stop the Darkness by ourselves," she said.

"What are you doing?"

She decided it wasn't worth responding in her head. None of them were going to get anywhere if this escalated into an argument.

"Ella is right, it doesn't matter why it was sent. It's here and it's not going away. Az and I have first-hand experience of it. It will not stop. It will destroy everything."

"It sounds as though you know more than you're letting on," Gavin said.

She tried not to flinch. She did. She knew the Darkness intimately. It had been inside her. She knew what it intended to do.

"The Darkness over took her to send a message," Ella said.

"You failed to mention that part," Gavin replied.

"It didn't seem important."

"Well, it is. If it took her over once, what's to say it won't do it again?"

Ella turned to Azrael and Alice.

"Has it?"

Alice looked up at her angel. His expression was tense, his eyes dark with frustration. She knew one way or another, they were going to have to admit the truth now. This meeting was never going to end well.

She turned back to Ella.

"It showed me a vision of what will come to pass," Alice said.

"That didn't answer her question. Has it taken you again?" Gavin asked.

"Don't."

I have no choice, Az. If we're not honest with them, then they won't help us. We can't do this alone. You know as well as I do the Darkness will take me.

"Yes."

"You're more than just a messenger to it, aren't you?"

"Alice, stop."

How could she? They had to know exactly what they were all up against.

"Yes."

"So that's why your aura is black," Ella said, taking a step back.

"And you knew?" Gavin said, turning to Azrael.

"What difference does it make whether he knew or not?" Alice said.

"What exactly are you?"

"Its vessel. It will wreak its havoc through me."

Silence descended over the room. Alice looked around at everyone in turn. Most of them were looking at her with interest. She didn't like the attention. Being the Darkness' vessel was not something she'd signed up for. She edged backwards, closer to her angel.

The next moment a cold hand wrapped around her neck, holding her a few feet off the ground. She grasped at it, finding her airway cut off. Gavin's cold, green eyes bored into hers. She wasn't sure if anyone else had noticed quite yet. He'd moved so fast that she'd barely had time to blink.

"You are a threat to us all," he said.

There was a low growl from behind them.

Azrael.

Alice closed her eyes. It was coming. A sick feeling coiled in her stomach. She tried to pull at Gavin's hand, but she was beginning to find it impossible to get oxygen in her lungs. The Darkness burnt in her veins. It pushed her down into herself.

It was here.

When her eyes opened, they were pools of black. The voice that left her mouth was not her own.

"Hello little vampire."

His eyes widened a fraction. She tried to push against the Darkness, but it dug its way into her mind, sealing her away from the world.

"Did you think I would allow you to kill my physical form?" it said.

"Let her go," Azrael said.

She turned her head. Azrael wasn't hiding any longer. He glowed, his green eyes dark with anger. He'd stopped short of donning his angelic armour, but he was magnificent nonetheless. The Darkness purred inside her at the sight of him. Alice wanted to reach out to him. To curl herself around him and never let go. The Darkness had taken her by force, but she was not willing to go down without a fight.

Get the fuck out of my head. I don't want you here.

The Darkness merely laughed. The sound echoed around her skull.

"There is no need to come to her rescue, angel. I assure you, she will not be harmed," it said.

Black smoke dripped from her fingers, coiling around Gavin's hand. He released her after a moment, hissing in pain. She landed with a thump on the floor and took two steps backwards.

"Little vampire, did you think it would be that easy?"

Gavin said nothing, merely staring at her with rage burning in his eyes. Alice knew vampires were strong, but none of them were a match for God's wrath.

"I see you, vampire. I know what it is you care about, or should I say who?"

Her black eyes fell on Daisy. Alice wanted to scream. She could see what the Darkness had planned inside her head. She felt sick to her stomach. If she had control of her body, she would be bent over hurling her guts up at the images flashing through her head.

No! They haven't done anything wrong. He was trying to protect the world by ending me. It's not their fault. Please stop. You can't do this. I won't let you.

The Darkness ignored her.

"You'd do well to keep silent unless you wish me to take away the only thing you've ever loved," it said.

Gavin's eyes flashed with fear. He took a step back, followed by another. His hand wrapped around Daisy's arm. The dark-haired girl looked up at him with confusion. He shook his head, pulling her closer to him.

"Give her back to me," Az said.

Alice turned to him, a smile on her lips.

"Poor little angel. Do you think I will give her up because you asked me to? Do you think He cares what you want?"

He reached out, pulling her to him. He stared down at her with sadness in his expression. Alice wanted desperately to tell him it would be okay. Smoke curled around the two of them, obscuring them from the others.

Az, I don't think you can hear me, but I'm still here. I'm still in here.

She imagined kicking the Darkness to the curb. She didn't want this. All she wanted was Az.

"Please," he whispered, his voice breaking on the word.

She wanted to cry. Her angel needed her. In desperation, she kicked out with her mind, trying to dislodge the claws in her head.

"Oh, aren't you just pathetic? Azrael, Death Bringer, you have been corrupted by human emotions."

He flinched.

Shut the fuck up. Don't you talk to him like that!

She kicked out again. Trying to tear away from the Darkness' grasp on her. It laughed in her head again.

"Poor little Alice. She isn't best pleased by my words."

"Let her go."

"I will let her go when I'm good and ready."

He cupped her face, drawing her closer. The Darkness didn't back away, it stared up at him, expressionless.

"Alice, I know you're still in there. I know you're trying to come back to me. I'm here. I'll always wait for you. I don't care what it says. I don't care if my feelings for you are human or pathetic. All I care about is you. All I need is you. You know how I feel about you. We belong to each other. It can't have you."

Her heart snapped in half. She needed him. She needed him so much it burnt in her chest. She could feel his power pressing against her. He was trying to cast the Darkness from her. Adding her own pressure to match him, she fought against it. She wasn't going to be its pawn.

"You cannot expel me."

He kept a hold of her. She knew he didn't care the Darkness was still inside her. Az only saw her. She could feel it. There was affection in his eyes. She'd seen it so many times before. It made her heart ache further.

"Why have you not destroyed the world yet?"

"He has not commanded me to."

"Then He's not ready for it to end. It means we have time."

The Darkness laughed. The sound rang in her head.

"Your time will run out soon. The next time I take her, it will be her last."

Chapter Seventeen

S moke billowed out of her mouth at an alarming pace. She pitched forward into Az's chest. He caught her, holding her close.

"Alice," he whispered.

She couldn't speak. All her emotions crashed down over her. She clutched him tightly, burying her face in his solid chest. The whole ordeal made her sick.

Az... I can't. I just can't.

He stroked her hair.

"Shh, I know."

"What the fuck was that all about?" Lukas interjected.

Alice didn't turn her head to look at the assembled supernaturals. She didn't want to be here any longer.

"That was the Darkness," Az said.

"I gathered that much. I was talking about you, it and her."

"He sent the Darkness because of what Lucifer and I did thousands of years ago when we were exiled from Heaven. Because of the rebellion. He has no mercy left for any of us. As for why He chose Alice, I cannot answer that, but make no mistake, I will not allow any of you to kill her and neither will the Darkness."

"I think the only person capable of destroying that thing is you."

Az's arms around her tightened.

"He's not wrong."

"Can we go please?" she whispered.

"I think we should continue this discussion at a later date," Az said.

There was a murmur of agreement from several of the assembled party.

"I'll text Alice tomorrow," Ella said.

Alice turned, peering at them with clear, grey eyes. Ella looked a little sad for her and the others had varying expressions of shock, horror and confusion.

Az tugged her away. There was nothing else any of them could say at that moment. Things had not gone well. She'd almost been strangled to death by a vampire and the Darkness making an appearance set everyone on edge. At the very least, they now understood the threat.

When they were outside, Az took to the skies with her wrapped up in his arms. She nuzzled his chest with her face.

I'm tired. All I want to do is curl up in bed with you.

"That can be arranged."

I just want you to hold me and never let go.

He clutched her tighter. Her heart hammered in her chest. Was it the right time to say those words? Would she get another chance? She shook herself internally. She had to stop over thinking it. If she wanted to tell him she loved him, then she should just do it and stop making excuses.

He only set her down when they reached the penthouse and led her into the bedroom. Instead of undressing her as a human would, he clicked his fingers and she was in her pyjamas within an instant. He pulled back the covers and pressed her onto the bed. She tugged him down with her. They both collapsed in a heap, tangled up in each other. She couldn't help giggling a little.

"I haven't heard you laugh all day," he said, grinning at her.

He leant towards her, pressing his lips to her forehead. When he moved back, she pouted. His smile grew wider.

"Did I kiss you in the wrong place?"

She nodded. He kissed her cheek. She let out a little mewl of protest.

"Where else could you want my lips?"

If you don't kiss me properly right now, I'm going to throw you out of this bed.

He moved, brushing his lips over hers.

"Az, please," she whispered.

He stared down at her, his breath mingling with hers. What she saw in his expression made her still, her heart pounding in her ears. His bright green eyes blazed with unconcealed adoration.

"Tell me you're mine," he said, his voice quiet.

"I'm yours."

"Tell me you belong to me."

"I belong to you."

He closed the distance. His mouth against hers was gentle, unhurried. She reached up, curling her fingers into his hair.

My beautiful angel.

"I belong only to you."

When he pulled away, his eyes still burnt with affection. She didn't think he wanted to talk about what just happened and neither did she.

"Az, can I ask you to do something for me?"

"Mmm... What is it you wish?"

"It's just with everything that's happened and all the shit that's coming, I want... I want to see my parents."

He plucked her glasses from her face, placing them on the bedside table.

"Then I will take you tomorrow."

"I didn't really mean tomorrow, but okay."

She was silent for a minute.

"How am I going to explain you to them? They don't know I broke up with Jason. I can't exactly tell them I'm dating an angel either."

His eyes glinted with mischief.

"Is that what we're doing? Dating?"

"You know I can't very well explain that we belong to each other in a way they can't possibly understand."

"I will pretend to be your human boyfriend if you wish it."

She snorted. Azrael. Her boyfriend. It sounded ridiculous.

"Is that funny to you?" he asked, eyebrow raised.

"I've never really thought of you as my boyfriend. I just see you as my angel. Besides, I didn't think you'd want me to put human labels on our relationship."

"For you, I'd do anything."

She felt her face burning with his words. The intensity of his gaze made her pulse spike.

"Now you're just being overly sweet. Where's my disparaging angel who hates humanity?"

He grinned, cupping her face and running his thumb along her bottom lip.

"He's got a bit lost since he discovered this exquisite human right here."

"Az..."

Her heart was in her mouth. She pulled him towards her for another kiss. Those three words were on the tip of her tongue again. Her love for him threatened to burst out of her chest. It burnt through her like wildfire.

I... Az...

"What is it?"

Don't leave, okay? Hold me all night. I only feel safe when you're with me.

He pulled away, kissing her forehead. He tugged the covers over them.

"I'll never let you go, Alice," he whispered.

They sat together, Azrael scowling as the train pulled into Penshurst station. She tugged him up off the seat.

"Why you insisted on us travelling this way is beyond me," he muttered.

"You know why."

They stepped out of the carriage together, fingers entwined. Her parents were standing on the platform, smiles on their faces. She almost broke into a run, dragging Az along behind her. She let go of his hand and launched herself into their arms.

"My little girl," her dad said.

"Mum, Dad, I'm so happy to see you."

"We've missed you, darling," her mum said.

She pulled away, stepping back. Her hand found its way into her angel's again. He gave it a little squeeze. She wasn't looking forward to the conversation about why she was with him and not Jason.

"And who have you brought with you?" her dad asked, his eyebrow raised.

"It is nice to meet you both. My name is Azrael."

"Oh, like the angel?" her mum asked.

Az looked down at Alice, question in his eyes. She had forgotten to mention that her parents were religious unlike her.

"Yes, Mum, like the angel."

"Well, I'm Susan and this is my husband, Mike. It's a pleasure to meet you too," her mum said, putting her hand out.

Az shook it before shaking her father's hand.

"Shall we go? Lunch is ready and I'm sure you're both hungry," her dad said.

They followed her parents to their Land Rover, getting settled in the back. Az scowled, a pout appearing on his lips.

"I hate cars."

She tried not to laugh. He really was out of his element. He looked distinctly uncomfortable, his long legs pressed up against the front seat. She reached out, taking his hand.

I'm sorry. You know I appreciate you doing this for me.

"You are a very lucky woman."

And didn't she know it. She smiled at him, lifting their entwined hands and kissing his. His expression softened. She could see the faint glow he emanated shining around him. He really was a sight to behold.

"So, Alice... Are we allowed to ask why you're not with Jason?" her mum said.

She tore her gaze away from her angel. She'd been expecting this question.

"Um, well... you see..."

"Jason cheated on her," Az said.

"He what?" her dad exclaimed.

Alice wanted to put her head in her hands. This was not how she envisioned having this conversation.

"It's been over for a while. I'm sorry I didn't tell you. I was embarrassed."

"Oh sweetie, that idiot never deserved you," her mum said, turning back to give her a sympathetic look.

"And now my daughter is with you?" her dad said, looking back at Az for a moment.

"Dad!"

"She is. I assure you, I care for your daughter and have no intention of hurting her," Az said.

Her dad nodded, turning back to the road. Alice almost breathed a sigh of relief. She gave her angel a grateful smile.

"Your mother is wondering how you managed to attract such a beautiful man."

Stop listening to their thoughts! Wait... what?

He grinned at her. She eyed her mum. Alice didn't think she was all that, but to have her own parent think such things stung a little. She would never understand Az's attraction to her.

"I could never want anyone but you."

She didn't respond to his thought. He squeezed her hand. She didn't pull hers away. Their entwined fingers grounded her. A reminder that the angel was hers and hers alone.

When they arrived at her parent's farm, her mum led them into the dining room and insisted they make themselves comfortable.

"Are you sure you don't want any help, Mum?" Alice asked.

"No. Let me and Dad handle it."

Her mum left them to sit down at the already made table. Az tugged her into his arms, pressing a kiss to her forehead.

"Do they approve of you?" she asked.

"Mmm, perhaps, it is too soon to tell."

"Tell me what they think."

"You told me to stop listening."

"Well, I want to know now."

He chuckled, clutching her tighter.

"Your father already prefers me to Jason and your mother is happy because you look happy."

"I prefer you to Jason too."

He tucked a finger under her chin. His eyes were glittering with amusement.

"Is that so?"

"Yeah, well, Jason wasn't quite as awe inspiring in the bedroom."

He shook his head, leaning towards her. Their lips were only inches apart. She could feel the dusting of his breath against her mouth.

"Is that the only reason?"

"No," she squeaked.

"Mmm, enlighten me."

Instead of answering, she closed the distance. Kissing him always felt like magic. Her skin tingled all the way down her spine. There was a cough from behind them. Alice sprang away from her angel, face flaming. Her mum stood in the doorway, her eyebrow raised. She had a dish in her hands. Alice immediately went over and took it from her.

"Let me get that," she said.

Her mum smiled at her and went back through to the kitchen. She placed it on the table and sat down, avoiding Az's intense gaze. He took a seat next to her, his hand resting on her thigh. He leant over, his mouth close to her ear.

"A little flustered, are we?"

"Shh, you."

His fingers danced up her inner thigh.

"Az, stop it," she hissed.

She pushed his hand away, aware of her body's immediate reaction to his touch. She wanted him to tear her clothes off and bend her over her parent's dining room table, but that was hardly appropriate.

"You have such a delicious imagination," he whispered. "Perhaps you can show me the farm later. I'm sure we can find somewhere to indulge in such activities."

Alice was sure her face was the colour of a tomato at that moment. She could think of a number of places to take him where her parents wouldn't see. The woods for a start. She'd wondered what it'd be like to have him take her up against a tree.

You're incorrigible!

"And you have got a very dirty mind, young lady. I'm not sure you'd want the bark digging into your back."

"Az, please. This isn't fair. Stop making me think about these things."

His breath fanned across her face, a deep rumble of laughter erupting from his chest. He drew away. There was footfall behind them.

"I hope you're hungry," her mum said.

Her dad bustled in carrying beef wellington. Alice looked over the table. They'd gone all out and made them a roast. She smiled. It'd been a long time since she'd had a home cooked meal at her parents. Az didn't usually eat during the day, but he'd taken to having dinner with her in the evenings to keep her company. He did human things for her sake. She appreciated it far more than she could ever put in words.

"Please help yourself," her mum said as she sat down.

When they were all seated and plates piled high, her dad turned to the two of them. Alice was immediately suspicious of the twinkle in his eye. Her father was never one to mince words. He'd out right asked what Jason's intentions were when she'd first brought him home before he'd had a chance to get through the door. She dreaded what kind of questions he might ask Az.

"So, Alice, if you and Jason are no longer together, where have you been staying?"

Chapter Eighteen

"With me," Az said immediately.

Alice wanted to crawl under the table and never come out. She didn't want her parents thinking she couldn't survive by herself. She was twenty-five now and should be independent.

"Dad, it's not what you think. I had nowhere to go after I broke up with Jason," Alice said.

Her dad raised his eyebrow. She should've spoken to Az about this before they came here.

"I did warn you about moving in with that boy," her dad replied.

She gripped Az's thigh under the table.

"Mike, leave her alone," her mum interjected. "Alice, dear, pass the green beans please."

Thankful for her mum's interruption, she did as she was asked, not meeting her parent's eyes.

"How did you the two of you meet?" her mum continued.

"Alice sat next to me on a park bench. I offered to take her for a drink when she told me about Jason, so she could have someone to talk to," Az said.

"And how did she come to live with you?" her dad asked.

Her mum gave him a sharp look.

"I offered her my spare room for the night, which then turned into weeks. Not that I objected to her staying."

Alice tried not to roll her eyes. He'd forced her to stay with him, but her parents didn't need to know that. She wasn't complaining about it. Az had kept her out of harm's way.

"I see and when did this turn into a relationship between the two of you?" She wanted to put a hand over her dad's mouth. It was all very well him being concerned for her welfare, but he could've asked her privately.

"It was a few weeks, Dad. He didn't do anything untoward. Can you stop giving us the third degree now, please?" Alice said.

Her dad grinned at her.

"As you wish, sweetie."

They lapsed into a silence, each concentrating on their meals, which Alice could only be glad of. She didn't want any further talk about their relationship.

When the conversation resumed, it was on more neutral ground. Her mum asked Az what he did. He gave her a vague answer about working in finance. Her dad wanted to know if he was into football and what team he supported. Alice grinned when he admitted to having no interest in team sports. Az was an angel. He didn't engage in many human pursuits.

After lunch, her mum ushered them out of the house and ordered Alice to take Azrael on a tour of the farm. Alice led him to the cow sheds first, showing him the milking barn and the paddocks where the cows grazed. They wandered through her mum's vegetable garden before Alice took him across some of the fields. There was a wooded area to their right. Az looked over at her, his expression mischievous.

"Didn't you have some ideas about the trees?" he asked.

"Azrael, can you get your mind out of the gutter for one afternoon?"

"When it comes to you? No."

He picked her up and tossed her over his shoulder. She squealed in protest.

"Put me down."

He strode towards the trees and into the woods.

"Az, please. This isn't funny. My parents will be expecting us back."

"Don't you want me?"

She was silent. He knew very well she wanted him, but now wasn't the time. He pressed her up against a tree, her legs wrapped around his waist. His intense expression made her pulse spike. His green eyes blazing with need.

"Az..."

"Tell me you don't want me to fuck you and we'll go back."

He ground into her. She whimpered in response. He leant towards her.

"What will it be... hard, fast and furious or do you want to be left wanting?"

You know the answer to that.

He smiled before claiming her mouth. He bit down on her lip, causing her to cry out.

"Mmm, that's right, Alice."

"Az..." she whimpered.

"Do you want me to continue?"

His hands were under her t-shirt, trailing along her sides.

I need you like I need air. I can't say no to you. You know that.

He buried his face in her neck, lips trailing along her skin. She gripped his shoulders. Her body was flaming. He knew all the right buttons to push.

"I'm not going to be gentle, sweet Alice. I'm going to give you exactly what you crave. I want to hear you scream for me."

She trembled, needing him to make good on his promises. He ground into her again. Their clothes needed to go. Right now. She couldn't take it any longer.

"Az, please. I want you to fuck me."

He growled in her ear. The sound reverberated across her skin.

"Well, am I interrupting something?" came a voice from behind them.

Az stiffened. She looked behind Az, finding his brother leaning up against a tree nearby. His wings were folded neatly behind his back. A smirk on his perfect face. She remembered him from when the Darkness had taken over her.

Lucifer. He is beautiful, but not in the same way as Az.

"What are you doing here?" Az asked, his voice tight.

"I merely want to speak to you. Since you almost never leave your sanctuary, now seemed like the most appropriate time," Lucifer replied. "It seems the two of you are... busy."

Az pulled away, settling Alice back down on the ground. He tucked her under his arm, turning towards his brother. Alice stared at the other angel. Or should she call him the Devil? Either way, she was wary.

"Talk."

"You know, I'm relatively sure this is not what Father intended when He made her the vessel."

"I do not recall asking your opinion."

Alice wrapped an arm around Az's waist.

"Are you not going to introduce me?"

"She knows who you are."

Lucifer looked Alice over, dark eyes glinting in the sunlight.

"Excuse my brother, he clearly has no manners. Lucifer: Morningstar, Devil and Archangel at your service."

He bowed deeply.

"Alice," she replied.

"Lucifer, now is not the time for pleasantries. What do you want?" Az said.

Lucifer rolled his eyes, taking a step towards them.

"Don't worry, Azrael, I have no intention of hurting your human. I value my own life far too much. No, I wish to work with you to stop the Darkness."

Alice looked from Lucifer to Az. Her angel was staring at his brother with a frown.

"Why have you suddenly changed your tune?"

"The Darkness threatens Hell as well as Earth."

"And yet I still see no reason for you to help me."

Lucifer's face hardened.

"The Gates of Hell are sealed. No new souls are arriving."

Az's expression darkened.

"Do you think it's the same for Heaven?"

Lucifer shrugged. This did not bode well.

"I imagine so. It means that Earth is saturated with spirits. This is only the beginning. The beginning of the end."

What does this mean? Are we running out of time?

He nodded slowly rather than responding to her question. All of her previous pent up desire vanished. She was going to lose the angel she loved. The Darkness told them the next time it came, it would be the last. Tears pricked at her eyes. She blinked them back. She would not cry in front of Lucifer.

"You wish to work with us?" Az asked.

"I wish to prevent the Darkness consuming everything."

Az was silent for a long moment. His fingers flexed on her arm. She wondered what he made of his brother's sudden change of heart. To her, it felt like he only changed his mind because his life in Hell was disrupted. Self-preservation rather than a genuine need to save the world.

Wouldn't surprise me in the slightest.

There was an odd wisp of darkness curling around his wings for a moment. When she blinked, it vanished. She frowned. There was no doubt in her mind. She'd most definitely seen that. A sticky feeling coated her skin. The Darkness. It was here yet it wasn't ready to take her just yet. She shivered. Az looked down at her for a moment. She shook her head. He didn't need to be worried about her right now.

"Fine. I assume you will bring your army of followers."

Lucifer nodded.

"Then be ready when I call."

His brother smiled thinly. Alice decided she didn't like the angel in front of her. Lucifer made her uncomfortable.

"Soon, Azrael. It will be soon."

He took a few steps backwards before he took off into the skies, leaving Alice and Az alone. She turned into him, wrapping her other arm around his back. He uttered a low growl of frustration.

"I don't trust him," she whispered.

"Good. You shouldn't."

"It won't be long. I can feel it."

Az wrapped his other arm around her, kissing the top of her head.

"What do you need?"

"Why would I need anything?"

"The end of the world is looming and you need nothing?"

She was silent. She had all she needed in front of her. That was the thing. Az had become her sole focus. Her angel.

"Help me forget about it then."

She felt a rumble of approval in his chest. He backed her up against the tree again, his fingers running down her sides.

"Mmm, are you sure we do not need to return to your parents?"

She looked up at him, eyes narrowed.

"Don't make me regret giving into you. In fact, just shut up and kiss me before I change my mind."

Tugging him down, their lips met. Explosions went off in her head. *Every. Single. Damn. Time.*

There wasn't anything left to say anyway. They both knew what was going to happen when the Darkness took her. If these were to be some of the last moments they shared, she wanted them to be passionate. A reminder that they belonged to each other in some inexplicable way.

I want you now. No teasing.

He uttered a low growl before the next moment they were both undressed. Picking her up, she wrapped her legs around him. He pressed her against the tree as he entered her. The bark dug into her back.

"I warned you. I'm not going to be gentle," he whispered.

She could feel him everywhere. He glowed with light. His full angelic nature coming to the forefront. His wings flared out from his back and a soft halo appeared above his head.

Beautiful. So fucking beautiful.

The pace he set was relentless. Her back ached, but the pain only intensified her pleasure. She wanted the rough sting of his brutal pounding and the tree bark digging into her skin. She wanted to feel it all as a reminder she was still alive. She held on for dear life, her fingers digging into his shoulders. It was everything she needed and yet almost not enough.

"Harder," she whispered. "I need more."

He backed them away from the tree. Setting her down, he pressed her onto all fours in the dirt before kneeling behind her. He pressed into her again, gripping her hips in an iron hold.

"More, Alice? Are you sure you can take more?" he asked.

"I want to feel alive. Only you can give that to me. Az... You're everything. My everything."

The sounds of their brutal love making rang through the forest. She cried out, fingers digging into the dirt. The pain, the pleasure overtook everything. Sweat beaded on her back.

"Is this what you want?" he grunted, clearly as affected as she was.

She looked back at him, eyes shining with unshed tears. He was still in his full angelic form. Wings flared out, a halo of light above his head. Her heart broke into a thousand tiny pieces. Her love for him consumed every inch of her being. If there was ever a time to admit the truth of it, it was now.

Yes, this is all I want. Just you and me together. My beautiful angel. I crave you in ways I never imagined possible. Forever, Az. I wish we had forever.

He released her hips, pulling her up so her back was flush with his chest. His breath fanned across her ear. His hands splayed out over her stomach, anchoring her to him.

"My sweet Alice, you will have me forever. Even when the Darkness comes. I will always be yours. We are bound. He knows that. He cannot keep us from each other."

Tears spilled over. She couldn't hold them back. A part of her wanted to believe him. How could she? The Darkness would take her form and destroy her in the process. The only God she knew was cruel and unjust. He'd cast out her angel from his home and forced him into a life he never wanted. He'd made her a vessel for his wrath. How could anyone call him a just and fair God after that?

She turned enough so she could kiss Az. Feeling the softness of his mouth against hers threatened to undo her all over again.

I want so much to tell you the words stuck inside me, but I can't.

"I know what you feel. I told you I feel it too. We don't need to say those words. It is enough that we feel this way about each other."

Flipping her around again, he pressed her down into the ground. They clutched each other, so close to the edge. Her legs wrapped around his back. His lips against her collarbone, kissing up towards her neck.

"I am yours," he whispered. "You are mine."

"Forever."

Meeting each other in an explosive climax, Alice screamed his name, shattering the peaceful silence of the woods. And the two of them lay spent together for a long time as the shadows grew longer. The afternoon light fading. Neither of them cared much about returning to the real world. Not when the real world was about to come to an end.

Chapter Nineteen

Alice stood in front of the mirror in the bathroom. Her hands placed on the counter by the sink. She stared at her reflection. For days she'd felt strange. She could've sworn she'd been seeing things. Smoke curled around her in the mirror, her eyes pools of never ending darkness.

She blinked rapidly, trying to clear the hallucination from her mind. It was still there, taunting her. It was coming. The Darkness. Sending her a clear message. Her time was almost up. She cursed.

"Alice?"

She jumped at the sound of his voice. His footsteps silent against the tiled floor. She eyed the mirror again, but the smoke was gone. He curled his arms around her waist, dropping a kiss on her shoulder.

"What is it?" Az asked.

"Nothing."

"It's not nothing. What did you see?"

"The smoke again. My eyes were black. Time has run out. I feel it."

She placed her hands on top of his. The silence enveloped the two of them. What else could she say? It was time. This day would always come. Nothing could stop the Darkness.

"Then let me make these last moments with you count," he whispered in her ear.

She turned in his arms. He pushed her up against the counter, his green eyes blazing with emotions she didn't want to understand. The time for talking was over. They'd admitted how they felt even if the words hadn't been uttered. What good would it do to say them out loud anyway? It would only make the inevitable unbearable. She let Az take her in the ways he wanted to because that's what they needed. It was the only way they could say goodbye to each other.

His kisses were gentle, his touch unhurried as if they had all the time in the world. And she supposed they did in a way. The Darkness would allow her one more moment of unadulterated bliss with him before it took her. It would never be enough, but it would have to be. She couldn't ask it for more.

In the aftermath of their union, he lay splayed out on the bed, his hand curled loosely around her waist. He'd fallen asleep. Her beautiful angel was dead to the world. Running her fingers through his auburn hair, she sighed. He almost never slept. The days spent worrying about when their last together would be had taken it out of him. It made her heart ache.

"Azrael," she whispered. "Thank you for the last few months. For caring for me. For your touch. For your affection. It never occurred to me anyone was able to feel the way I do about you. Bound to one another in a way no one else could ever understand. I wish that we had forever. I never wanted to let you go. Az... fuck."

Tears dripped down her cheeks. She was tired of crying, but it was all she could seem to do.

"I love you."

The weight on her shoulders lifted slightly. Even if he was sleeping, she'd managed to voice her feelings out loud.

"I'll always love you, from now until the very end."

There was a rushing sensation in her head. It was here. Its laughter rang in her ears.

"Silly girl. Did you think your love for him would change anything?"

"No. If you're here to take me, then at least allow me to kiss him one last time."

There was silence in her head. She leant down, pressing her lips to his. Her tears fell down onto his cheeks. She stifled a sob when she pulled away. She rested her fingers on his cheek, brushing away the wetness. She didn't want him knowing she'd cried when she said goodbye.

"Remember I love you, Az. You'll know it when you wake up. You'll feel it every day for eternity. You have to go on without me. Please don't give up.

Please don't let yourself drown in sorrow. I love you, my beautiful angel. Goodbye, Azrael. My Archangel of Death."

She crawled off the bed. The Darkness became an almost solid form in front of her. It was her image in black smoke. It smiled at her. She felt the sticky feeling rake across her skin again. There wasn't anything she could say to it. Whatever words she had left were gone. Her heart was torn to shreds.

"It is time you and I ended the world, Alice."

Azrael jerked awake. He felt an ache deep in his chest. Eying the empty bed beside him, he frowned. She should be here. He jumped up, tearing through the penthouse. Alice was gone. The knowledge of it almost made him collapse in the middle of the living room floor. He felt the whisper of her touch against his cheek.

"Alice," he whispered, choking on the word.

He'd never wanted to feel human emotions, but they came crashing down on him all at once. Despair raked through him, tearing his insides to pieces. His heart tightened in his chest. His legs finally gave out. He knelt on the floor as a single tear slipped down his cheek. The Darkness had come and taken her from him.

"Why, Father? Why have you done this to me? Why did you give her to me only to take her away?"

There was only one person he could blame for this cruelty. His father. Yet if he hadn't thrown Lucifer and Azrael out of Heaven, he would've never had the chance to meet Alice. To love her in the way he did.

It didn't mean he had to like what had happened now. This was too much. All he wanted was to see her face again. To hold her in his arms. They'd not had enough time. Forever would never be enough. Tears streamed down his face. He no longer cared. Nothing mattered now she was gone.

"Azrael," a voice whispered inside his head. *"Do not fail me now."*

It was not just any voice. It was the voice of God. Of his father. He looked up at the ceiling, confusion marring his features.

"Fail you? How have I failed you now?"

"The end is coming, Azrael. Your purpose on Earth. You must fulfil your duty."

"What if I don't care anymore? You've taken everything from me."

"Have faith, my son."

Then there was only silence. Silence which rang in his ears.

Faith? What is the point in having faith? Why are you always so cryptic? You and Lucifer have that in common.

It had always driven him crazy. Lucifer had always been his father's son. His favourite. None of them had ever matched up to the love their father had for his Morningstar. And yet, his favourite had disappointed him the most. Lucifer was sent to rule over Hell as punishment for his disobedience.

Lucifer would always be God's favourite child. Azrael knew this because of the expression their father had worn when he'd cast them out. The pain in his eyes was unpalatable. It wasn't for Azrael, but for the Morningstar. The brightest of all is creations. Now, Lucifer was the darkest of them all.

He felt something calling to him. A whisper in the air.

"I am waiting, Azrael. You know where to seek me. You know where you'll find her."

A tight feeling echoed around his chest. The Darkness sought him. He knew exactly where it was hiding. Waiting for him. It was time he ended things. He dreaded every moment. The Darkness would be wearing her face. He almost couldn't stand it.

He rose to his feet. The sun dipped in the sky. Dusk was coming. He found Alice's phone on the bedside table. He sent one message.

It's time. The Darkness is here.

He slipped it into a pocket. Ella would want to know where they needed to assemble. He stepped out of the penthouse, ghosting through the window as if it wasn't even there. His wings flared out before he flew upwards and landed on the roof. Through the bond angels shared, he called to his brother. Minutes later, Lucifer landed with a thump on the roof.

"It is time," Azrael said.

"I felt it too. You know where it is to end?"

Azrael nodded. Lucifer gave him a tight smile before taking to the skies again. They both knew what was expected. He stood for several moments. Would he ever be prepared to see the Darkness wearing the face of the woman he loved?

He jumped off the roof, allowing the wind to carry him towards the place where everything would end. Alice's phone buzzed in his pocket. He pulled it out mid-flight.

Where?

He fired back a quick message to Ella. He knew they would come. They would bring whoever they could. He could see the park below him. There was a clearing. He soared towards it, landing with a thump. His wings tucked behind him as he looked around. He could feel its presence everywhere, permeating the air. The sky darkened at an alarming pace.

Lucifer landed beside him. He glanced at his brother. Lucifer's expression was hard. Large cracks formed in the ground and up rose several higher demons. Azrael stiffened. The scent of them made his nostrils flare. He hated demons, but now was not the time for old divisions. They had a common enemy.

"Where is she?" Lucifer asked.

"It took her. Can't you feel it in the air?" Azrael responded.

Lucifer's expression soured further. Who'd have thought they would be standing here again? Brothers in arms once more. United against the Darkness. The shadows shifted next to them and out walked Gavin, Neave and Jack. Ella had worked fast. He imagined they'd been recognising the signs the Darkness was here for days. They would've been prepared for this moment. But where were the two angel, demon hybrids?

Gavin nodded at Azrael. He was still a little wary of the vampire after Gavin had tried to kill Alice. He was sure the Darkness had not forgotten that little incident either. Perhaps that's why he hadn't brought Daisy with him. The vampires looked over at where the demons were still assembling, eyes growing wide before glancing over at the angel standing next to Azrael.

"Is that...?" Neave whispered to Jack.

"Oh, that most definitely is," Jack replied.

"Shit. Didn't expect him to look so... ethereal."

"He is an angel, Neave."

Neave jabbed Jack in the side, scowling.

"Ha, fucking point out the obvious why don't you?"

Azrael wanted to shake his head at their interaction. Now wasn't the time for jokes. Beyond the three vampires, more started to pop up as they slowed down from their run.

A little way off a purple light appeared. Out walked Grace followed by Dalia and the werewolves he'd met at The Werehouse and several others. Lastly, the witch, Alistair walked through with two other men who looked to be twins and the portal disappeared. The only two missing from the assembled party of shifters were Izzy and Rex. It didn't surprise him considering the female werepanther was heavily pregnant.

There were two loud thumps besides him and Lucifer. He glanced over at the noise. Ella and Lukas had arrived, both of them with their wings extend and horns protruding from their foreheads. Ella set Daisy down. She stormed over to her husband who looked at her in shock.

"You shouldn't be here," Gavin said.

"Do you think I'm going to be left out of the world ending? Are you crazy?" Daisy replied.

"But my love—"

"Don't you start with me, Gavin. I am not leaving."

She reached out to him, cupping his face with one hand.

"My heart is here, with you. Always. You know that."

Gavin pulled her two him, holding the dark-haired girl close.

"You are the most infuriating woman."

"Yet you love me anyway."

There was a small smile playing on his lips at her assertion.

"You need to stay back, Daisy."

She put her hand out. Ella threw something at her. She caught the bright dagger deftly.

"As if you think I'd come here without anything to defend myself with. Ella has been teaching me, as you well know."

The vampire shook his head before releasing her.

"My wife, fiery as ever."

"You know it."

Azrael's attention was drawn away to the treeline. A woman emerged with a long, flowing black dress on. She had black eyes and wore a sneer on her perfect lips. Behind her, black smoke pooled, wisps twisting and turning besides her. She was the reason they were here. She was still as beautiful now as the day he'd first seen her. His heart lurched.

"Alice," he whispered.

Chapter Twenty

lice walked towards them with slow measured steps. She left behind black scorch marks in her wake from her footsteps. Azrael knew it wasn't her any longer, but it didn't stop him wanting to go to her. His feet moved of their own accord before anyone could stop him. She was still everything to him. His Alice. Something shifted behind her black eyes. Something which gave him far more hope than he should ever strive to possess.

Alice stopped halfway towards the assembled group. A frown appeared on her brow. Her eyes fell on Az. She put a hand on her heart as if she was feeling something alien. He didn't hesitate, striding over to her with determined steps. Alice blinked rapidly when he stood in front of her. Her black eyes cleared. Those perfect grey eyes appearing in their stead.

"Az?" she whispered. "Are you... are you really here?"

He reached out, cupping her face, running a thumb along her cheek.

My love.

"Yes."

"I don't know how long I can keep it at bay."

She shuddered, the smoke coiling around her. She shook it off.

"How are you still in there? It took you from me."

His heart pounded so hard he felt as though it might burst through his chest. She was still here. She was still alive. His Alice.

"I don't know. When it saw you, it couldn't keep me out. I can see everything it sees. Feel everything it feels. It is almost as if we are linked to each other. The Darkness cannot exist without me."

Azrael froze, the implications of what she was saying dawning on him. He didn't like it. Not one bit. Yet she was standing in front of him. The woman he loved with every inch of his being. The Darkness hadn't destroyed her. Not yet.

"Alice, I thought... I thought I'd never see you again. I thought I would only see the Darkness wearing your face."

She gave him her brightest smile. *Radiant.* She had always been the most perfect woman to him.

"I can't keep this up, Az. I'm sorry."

Tears slipped down her cheeks. He brushed them away. He took her hand, placing it directly on his chest where his heart lay. He placed his own on top of hers.

"This is yours."

"Az," she said, choking on his name.

"It has always been yours. I will never feel this way about another."

She brought her other hand up, placing it on his, where he could feel her heart pounding.

"And mine is yours."

Her eyes flickered from black to grey. He was losing her again. He leant down, their lips brushing for a mere moment. When he pulled away, her eyes were black again. She smiled at him.

"Azrael," the Darkness spoke through her perfect mouth. "Your little human girl is going to watch me burn the world."

He was shoved backwards, flying through the air until he slammed into someone else. They fell backwards with Azrael sprawled out on top of his brother.

"Get off me," Lucifer grunted, shoving at Azrael's back.

He rolled off his brother, getting up and dusting himself down. Lucifer sprung up, rage burning in his dark eyes.

"That was not a smart idea, brother," he said, his words dripping with disdain.

"What would you have me to do? The Darkness has taken her form."

"Your feelings for that human girl will be our downfall."

Azrael clenched his fists. Lucifer was already getting on his nerves. An alliance with his brother was never a good idea. No after the centuries had soured their relationship.

"You couldn't possibly understand."

"No, I suppose not. I do not concern myself with mortal emotions. They're useless. And yet they will prevent you from doing what you're meant to."

"What's that supposed to mean?"

"What did Father say to you?"

Azrael paced away. Alice was still standing watching the assembled crowd with an expression of glee on her face.

"Does it matter? He told me I had to fulfil my purpose no matter what."

"Only you can end this. Don't you see? None of us will be able to do it."

He looked at the woman he loved. He knew what Lucifer was getting at. The end. His father said he would bring the end. Azrael had always thought he meant the end of the world, but perhaps he was wrong. Perhaps his real destiny was to bring an end to the Darkness.

A prospect he did not relish in the slightest.

He would have to kill Alice in order to destroy the Darkness.

It was the only way to save the world from ruin.

And it would tear his heart and soul to shreds in the process.

Alice felt the Darkness commanding every inch of her body. She was frozen inside. Utterly helpless. Those last few moments she'd been able to speak to Az were too much for her. She'd already said her goodbyes. She thought the Darkness would destroy her. It could inhabit her body, but Alice was still here. She felt herself rising up, huge black wings of smoke coiled around her back.

"The time has come. You who stand in my way will be cast down," the Darkness said.

You know, you sound like a cartoon villain right now.

The Darkness ignored her. Black smoke poured out of her fingers, coiling around until there were at least a hundred solid smoke figures below her. The demons were the first to engage, roaring as they ran towards the figures, swinging swords and battle axes. The vampires and wolves followed. Azrael and Lucifer stayed back. She hadn't expected the two of them to engage. They seemed to be arguing with each other instead. She wanted to know what they were saying, but she was too far away and the battle cries were too loud.

The Darkness laughed, the sound echoing around her head.

Evil laughs are also cartoonish. Are you really that one dimensional? You might have control of my body, but I'm not some pawn in your games.

"Oh, dear Alice, but you are."

She shoved at the Darkness, wanting it out of her body. She knew it was useless to try, but it didn't stop her. This sick game it was playing made her heart ache. God's Wrath. She couldn't help but feel God was holding back a little. All this talk of destroying the world and yet there was no real evidence it was what he actually intended.

If God really wanted to destroy everything, He could do it without sending you. Tell me, why are you really here?

"You ought not to think too much on it. It's not your concern. You are merely my vessel. You cannot stop this from happening."

Nothing good was coming out of her arguing with the Darkness. She observed the ensuing battle. Demons, vampires and shifters clashed with smoke figures. She couldn't tell who was winning and who wasn't. The witches started to engage, throwing spells at the figures approaching the two angels, Ella, Lukas and Daisy.

Lucifer and Azrael were still deep in conversation, ignoring the battle completely. Out of the corner of her eye she saw the three vampires she'd met fighting back to back in a defensive stance. The Darkness seemed to notice her interest.

"Ah, that vampire. Now, where is his little wife?"

Don't. Don't you dare!

Images of what the Darkness intended to do to Daisy flashed through her mind. She wanted to scream. It was horrific. She might not have trusted Gavin, but she didn't want the Darkness to kill an innocent human either.

The Darkness reached out a long arm of smoke, coiling through the crowd until it hit its target standing beside Ella and Lukas. It whipped her upwards. A scream rang out.

"Get the fuck off me," Daisy shouted, trying to desperately shove the dark smoke off her.

Stop. Just stop. She doesn't deserve any of this.

Daisy was hanging upside down, her dark hair falling down in waves. The smoke had latched on to one of her feet. Alice tried to push against the Darkness again. It laughed in her head.

I hate you. You're ruining all our lives and for what? Because God commanded you? That's bullshit.

"Oh, little vampire, look who I've found," the Darkness said, its attention on Gavin.

Gavin turned looking up at the Darkness with a frown. His eyes followed the line of smoke widening when they fell on Daisy.

"No," he shouted.

He ran towards her, fighting his way through the mass of bodies and smoke.

"Daisy!"

"Gavin," she shouted, twisting around to look at him. "Don't do anything stupid."

The Darkness laughed.

"Little human, your life is wasted on him. Vampires are abominations. Yet, you still seek to stay with the man who almost got you killed."

"Shut the fuck up," Daisy said. "What the fuck do you even know anyway?"

"I've seen inside your head, little human."

"Then you'll know he's changed. He loves me and I love him. What does it even matter to you anyway?"

"Why, nothing."

And with that, the Darkness threw her across the clearing. She flew into a tree, an almighty smack sounding before she slumped down in front of it. The Darkness turned its attention back to the battle, but Alice was focused on the vampires and Daisy.

No! No! She can't be dead.

Daisy raised her head slightly. She opened her mouth. Blood pooled out of it. A roar of anguish sounded. Neave and Jack turned their heads, spying Daisy by the trees. They zipped towards her just as Gavin arrived at her feet. He knelt down, cupping her face.

"Gavin," she choked out.

"Shh, my love, it's okay. I'm here."

"This feels a little like déjà vu."

"Don't say that."

She half smiled at him.

"Did you ask her?"

He shook his head.

"Well, now she won't have a choice."

Alice had no idea what they were referring to, but she knew on some level, Daisy was dying. It wasn't right. She'd done nothing.

Neave and Jack arrived next to Daisy and Gavin. He looked up at the female vampire.

"She doesn't look good, boss," Neave said.

Jack eyed Gavin for a moment before nodding.

"I need you to do something for me, Neave," Gavin said.

"What?"

"Turn her."

Neave's eyebrows shot up. She took a step back.

"No. Hell no. You know I don't want to be anyone's sire. You know why. Don't make me do this."

Daisy's head lolled on her chest. She'd fallen unconscious.

"If I do it, our relationship will change and neither of us want that. Please, Daisy is willing. We've talked about this. It has to be you."

Neave looked between Daisy and Gavin. Alice didn't know what a relationship between a vampire and their maker entailed. Azrael hadn't told her much about the supernatural world.

"Why not Jack?"

"You know why," Jack replied. "I'm returning to Peru with her brother."

Neave looked sceptical for a moment. She sighed. She knelt down on the floor besides Gavin, taking Daisy's arm and pulling it towards her.

"Are you sure this is what she wants?" Neave asked.

"Yes. Save my wife. Please."

Neave bit down on Daisy's wrist. Alice flinched internally. She didn't really want to watch a blood exchanged. She imagined it was what Neave was going to do. She couldn't think of another way that a vampire could create another. If this was the only way to save Daisy, she could only be glad of it. It would rob the Darkness of its revenge against Gavin in some small way.

Minutes ticked by until Neave released Daisy's wrist.

"How much blood do I need to give her?" she asked.

"I don't know. I've never made another vampire," Gavin replied.

"And yet you expect me to do it. Men. Typical."

Gavin smiled at her. Neave tore open her wrist with her teeth before clasping Daisy's head and tipping it back. Neave opened Daisy's mouth and put her wrist to it. Alice couldn't make out exactly what was happening, but she imagined blood was dripping down. After a minute, Neave had to re-open the wound at her wrist.

"How will I know when it's taken?" Neave asked.

"You'll feel it. At least that's what I've been told."

Neave frowned but turned back to Daisy. She looked very pale to Alice's eyes. Neave seemed to stiffen for a moment before pulling her wrist back.

"It's done," she said.

"Now you have to take her to ground," Jack said.

"Seriously? And this is a new outfit."

She leant down and picked up Daisy.

"I trust you, Neave," Gavin said. "Take care of my wife."

Neave rolled her eyes. Gavin stroked Daisy's hair from her face, placing a kiss on her cheek. He stepped back and Neave sped away. Alice could only hope that Daisy survived.

Gavin turned, looking up at the Darkness with a thunderous expression on his face. Alice knew without a doubt; the vampire would show no mercy. Not when it had tried to kill the woman he loved.

Chapter Twenty One

*H*is argument with Lucifer was getting them nowhere whilst the battle raged on around them. Azrael turned away, looking up at where the Darkness was possessing the woman he loved. He knew Alice was still in there watching this play out helplessly. His fists clenched at his side.

"You could've ended this a long time ago," Lucifer said.

"Just shut up. I'm done talking about this."

There was an ear-splitting scream. Azrael looked over at the source. Daisy was dangling in the grasp of the Darkness. There wasn't much he could do because there was another commotion next to him. A huge demon had grabbed hold of one of Ella's wings and was dragging her away.

"Lukas," she shouted.

Lukas whipped his head around. Rage contorted his features. He strode after the demon, his wings flaring out. Azrael's eyes narrowed.

"Who is that?" he asked Lucifer.

His brother looked over at the demon.

"Her father."

"Can you not keep your demons under control?"

"Let her go," Lukas said as he grabbed hold of Ella's hand after half flying, half striding over to Ella and the demon.

"You are interfering," the demon said.

"I'm not interested in coming with you," Ella said.

"I don't care. It was never meant to be this way."

"Beleth, let her go," Lukas said, his eyes glowing blue and red.

The demon chuckled.

"Should you not be battling the Darkness, Lukas?"

"Not without her. You can't have her. You're not worthy of your daughter."

Lucifer looked down at his hands.

"That is not my problem," he said.

Azrael growled. Lucifer was never one to care about anyone else but himself. He'd always been like this. Azrael took two steps forward before he felt something. Something he'd not experienced in centuries. He looked up at the sky. Hundreds of them. His brothers and sisters littered the sky. Their angelic armour glinted in the dying light. It would've been a sight to behold if any humans were witness to it.

"Well, that's just great," Lucifer exclaimed.

An angel they both knew well landed right next to Ella, Lukas and Beleth.

"I've warned you a thousand times. Let go of our daughter."

Beleth laughed again.

"Your threats are meaningless, Ariel."

"Her threats may be meaningless, but mine aren't," came the commanding tones of an angel Azrael never thought he'd see again.

He turned, finding three angels standing nearby. Their halos shining brightly, swords by their sides and white wings tucked behind their backs.

"And why am I not surprised they've turned up?" Lucifer said, rolling his eyes.

"Shut up," Azrael said.

The three angels turned at the sound of their voices.

Michael. Raphael. Gabriel.

"Brothers," Michael said, his golden hair glinting even in the dying light.

Azrael had no words.

"Tsk, they're here to take all the glory," Lucifer muttered.

"For the last time, why can't you just behave in a civilised manner?" Azrael said, turning on his brother, green eyes blazing.

"Are you going to fight me again? You know how well that went last time?"

"Honestly, I wish you would just go back to Hell where you belong."

Azrael stalked away towards his fellow Archangels. They looked the same as they had the day he'd been cast from Heaven.

"What are you doing here?"

"I am here to see my son," Michael replied.

Azrael's footsteps faltered.

His son? What?

"And to ensure you fulfil your purpose."

"It is nice to see you," Raphael said.

The angel was dark skinned with dark hair, his eyes golden. He smiled at Azrael. He'd never had a problem with Raphael or Gabriel.

"And you," Azrael replied. "Although the circumstances are less than fortuitous."

"Agreed, brother. It has been an age."

Gabriel, tanned with a crown of golden hair to match Michael and hazel eyes, strode towards Azrael before embracing him.

"Brother," he said.

Azrael stood stiffly for a moment before Gabriel released him. He did not like contact with others. The only person he wished to hold was currently possessed.

"Gabriel," Azrael replied.

"You look well."

Small talk amongst Archangels. Typical bullshit.

"What did you mean, your son?" Azrael asked, turning to Michael.

Michael took two steps towards where Beleth was still holding Ella. Ariel looked thunderous and Lukas was barely containing his fury.

"Let her go, Beleth," Michael said. "I'm sure you're aware of who I am and what I will do you to if you do not comply."

Beleth growled but released Ella. He slunk backwards into the shadows before disappearing into the earth again. Michael turned to Lukas, his blue eyes shining with pride. The realisation dawned on Azrael all at once. Even Michael had been involved in the creation of the hybrid angels and demons.

"My son," Michael said.

Lukas frowned, his arm curling around Ella's waist.

"What?"

"Have you never wondered who created you?"

"No. It didn't seem relevant after... after her."

Lukas looked down at Ella. It was clear as day, the two hybrids adored each other. Azrael could see their entwined souls burning inside each other. It was undeniable. They were made for each other.

"Allow me to properly introduce myself. I am the Archangel Michael. I am responsible for your existence. Both of you really."

Ella and Lukas frowned.

"What do you mean?" Lukas asked.

"Ariel could not do any of this alone. She is only a Guardian Angel. There were others, but none quite like the two of you."

"Wait, the actual Michael?" Ella interjected.

Michael smiled, giving her a slight nod. She nudged Lukas.

"I think you should at least hear him out."

Lukas gave her a squeeze before letting go and indicating with his head to Michael that they should go talk. The two of them walked off together.

"Who'd have thought pure and innocent Michael would stoop to such levels?" Lucifer muttered.

Azrael turned to his brother, scowling.

"And shouldn't you be dealing with that?"

Lucifer pointed towards the battle raging on next to them.

"Shouldn't you?" Azrael retorted.

"As I've already theorised, you are the only one who can end this. Here and now. Your feelings for that girl are preventing you from doing so."

Azrael knew Lucifer was right and it made him hate his brother even more. He turned towards the battle. This was on him. He knew what he had to do. His wings flared out and he took to the skies. He narrowly avoided the wisps of smoke permeating the air, moving ever closer to the Darkness and its vessel.

Demons clashed with smoke people. Werewolves weaved in and out, pouncing on their prey. Vampires flitted one from one place to another. Angels in their shining armour kept the Darkness back. At the very least, this was contained to one place. Azrael could not imagine if the Darkness spread across all of the Earth and what it would do if it razed through Heaven and Hell. But he'd seen it in Alice's visions. He could not allow that fate to come to pass.

The Darkness whipped its head around at his approach.

"So, the angel comes to claim his prize?" it said.

"Prize? You think this is my prize?"

"You want the girl back, do you not?"

His heart ached at the thought of Alice. He wanted her with every inch of his being. Clenching his fists, he scowled.

"You're not going to give her to me so what is the use in discussing it?"

The Darkness raised an eyebrow at him. It was disconcerting.

"Then what do you want?"

"To end this once and for all."

The Darkness smiled at him, black eyes pools of hatred.

"You think that's possible? You can barely look at me without seeing her. How do you propose you end it? If you kill me, you'll kill her too."

The pain in his chest was unlike anything else. He knew what he had to do, but it would cleave his heart in two. This conversation had gone on long enough. He reached out, gripping the Darkness by the arm and pulling it away from the battle. Her eyes widened as he set them down away from everyone else.

"You think this will stop me, angel?" it said.

"I don't care. I will not allow you to destroy everything."

His sword appeared. The Darkness smiled again. The next moment, its eyes cleared and there, standing before him, was the woman he loved.

"Az?" she whispered.

He faltered, unable to move. She was standing there with wide eyes.

"Are you... is it you?"

"I can't move, but yes, it's me," Alice replied.

His sword disappeared. He closed the distance, tugging her into his arms. He buried his face in her hair.

"Alice," he whispered. "My sweet Alice."

"Az... I know what you have to do."

"Shh, let me hold you for a moment."

His heart burnt in his chest. There wasn't much time left.

"You have to end it. It's okay. Please. I can't live like this. I don't want to watch it burn the world using me."

He clutched her tighter. Tears threatened to spill out. He didn't want that for her either. He kissed the top of her head.

"I'm sorry. I know. I won't make you live like this even if it kills me."

"I wish we had one more night with each other. I know I can't ask for forever, but I want you one last time. And yet I can't even have that. Instead you have to do the unspeakable. How is He this cruel?"

He could feel her tears soaking through into his shirt. Each word she spoke brought a new round of pain. He wanted to shout at his father. She was right. He wasn't even sure how God could be this cruel. Hadn't he done enough? Hadn't he taken everything from Azrael already? When would it be over?

"Look at me," she whispered.

He pulled away, staring down into her beautiful, tear-filled grey eyes.

"There's one thing I haven't told you."

He brushed her hair from her face.

"I love you, Azrael."

A single tear slipped down his cheek.

"And I love you, Alice."

She gave him a watery smile. A white dagger appeared in his hand.

"Now," she whispered.

Her eyes pooled black again. The Darkness looked at him with an expression he never thought he'd see. Fear. The dagger slipped between her ribs with ease until it connected with her heart. He felt blood trickle down his hand.

The ear-splitting screech emitted from Alice was inhuman. Her head fell back. Smoke billowed out of her, shooting upwards into the sky. Azrael didn't dare look around. He was staring down at Alice, who's eyes opened. They were grey again. She coughed twice.

"Goodbye," she said.

He dropped to his knees, clutching her to him as he pulled the dagger free. Tossing it away, he healed the wound.

"No, you can't leave me," he whispered.

"I'm sorry."

She reached up, cupping his face.

"My angel. You saved the world."

Her eyes closed.

"No."

He felt it when she died. The pain ripped through his chest. Alice was gone. Tears fell freely. Agony lanced every inch of his body and soul. The woman he belonged to had left him.

"No," he whispered. "No. I won't let you go. I won't let you leave me. Alice. You can't. I love you. I love you till the end."

There was nothing left for him without her. There were footsteps behind him. If someone was here to talk to him, he didn't want to hear it. Nothing any of them could say would make this pain disappear.

"Azrael," Michael said.

"What could you possibly want?" he snapped back.

"Your purpose on Earth. It is done."

"And that is supposed to make me feel better about killing her?"

Michael was silent. Azrael didn't look at him. He didn't care about anything anymore. He picked Alice up. His wings flared out before he took to the skies. If his purpose was done, then there was only one person in this world who could give him Alice back. The higher he flew, the more determined he became. He was responsible for all of this. He had created the Darkness and forced Azrael to murder the woman he loved.

He'd thought about returning to this place many times but seeing the Gates of Heaven again made his head hurt. Nestled in the clouds were two large, white doors. He landed on the cloud before it. They were closed. He knelt down, placing Alice before them.

"Father, if you have any love for me, for your son, give her back to me. Please. I have never asked anything from you. Even when Lucifer and I defied you, it was he who wanted freedom. I wanted to end my suffering. Watching all of them die. It was too much. And yet, even that does not compare to this."

He rested his hand on Alice's chest, above her heart.

"You know how we felt about each other. I am hers. Please, I am begging you. Give her back to me. I don't care if this isn't what you wanted. You've already taken everything from me. Why did it have to be her? Why did you make me kill the woman I love? When will it be enough? When will you allow my suffering to end?"

He could barely get the words out without breaking down and sobbing.

"Please, Father. Please bring her back."

His wings drooped. His head bowed.

"Please."

He clasped his hands together in prayer.

"I beg you, Father. Let her live again."

Chapter Twenty Two

he world seemed to come into focus all at once. She opened her eyes. It was so light in the room, it almost blinded her. She blinked rapidly.

Where am I?

Sitting up, she looked around. She was lying in an enormous bed. White billowing drapes fell down the sides from the four posts above her. Everywhere she looked, the room was white. White furniture. White marble floors. White doors.

Doors. They must lead out of this room.

She hopped off the bed, staring down at the long white flowing dress somebody had put her in. Placing her hand on her chest where she'd felt the dagger pierce her heart, she found there was no trace of a wound.

What happened to me? Am I dead? Is this… is this Heaven?

She needed answers. There was nothing for it. She walked over to the doors, her bare feet whispering on the floor. Pushing it open, she stepped out into a huge open space. There was nothing above them but dashes of blue and clouds. Surrounding the room were huge windows with white, flowing curtains to match the ones that were on the bed.

There was a man in white standing with his back to her. His hands were folded behind him, his brown hair cropped short. She took two steps towards him, faltering when she noted there was a man on his knees beyond him. Her chest tightened, heart pounding in her ears.

"Az," she whispered.

She broke into a run but was brought up short by the man in white's voice.

"He cannot hear you."

"What?"

"He is unaware of your presence because you and I need to have a conversation."

"Who are..."

She stopped. Staring at the back of the man's head, it dawned on her. She was in the presence of God himself.

"Yes, dear girl, I am the Creator."

Her eyes fell on her angel. His tear streaked face tore at her heart. She wanted to wrap her arms around him. Hold him until his tears faded. She wanted Az so much it hurt.

"Why is he crying?"

"He thinks you are dead. He is begging me to return you to him. I did not think I would see my son this way."

"Am I dead?"

"You were."

She wasn't sure what to say or do. Why would God want a conversation with her? And why had he brought her back for this? Was he going to allow her to be with Azrael like she desperately wanted?

"My son loves you. He has devoted himself to you and only you."

"You sound surprised."

"It is not what I intended. You see, Azrael needed to learn his place. To understand why he was given his duty. He carries souls to their resting place. He was tired of bringing death to your world."

She wasn't quite sure how to respond. She still thought his methods were cruel and unjust. Az hadn't deserved any of it.

"You would not understand why I chose to punish him in this way. Lucifer had too much influence over him. But that is not what I wished to speak to you of."

"Then what?"

She paced away, unable to look at her angel any further. His suffering caused her physical pain. She felt helpless, utterly powerless to give Azrael the comfort he needed. To reassure him she was alive.

"Your influence over my son was unexpected. Yet, you are the very reason he has returned home. He fulfilled his purpose, but I fear he will not continue his duty if I do not return you."

He took a step away from Az, keeping his back to her.

"He was not supposed to fall in love with you. You were a means to an end."

"I wouldn't expect anything less from you," she muttered, not caring if he heard her or not.

All she wanted was for this conversation to end.

"Tell me, why do you care for my son?"

"Don't you know the answer to that already?"

He was God. Didn't he know everything already? Why was he asking such a question?

"Explain it to me in your own words."

Turning again, she stared at Az. Her heart contracted in her chest. He looked so broken. She closed the distance between them. She knew he couldn't see her, but being so close to him set her skin on fire. She just had to get through this conversation and then, maybe God would finally allow her to be with her angel. He was hers and nothing would ever change that.

"I love him. Beyond all reason or explanation. He is the world to me. We saw each other for who we really are. He has suffered through an eternity of pain. By making me the vessel, you allowed me to see all angels for what they are, but with Az, it's different. Somehow, whatever you did, it bound us to each other. Can't you see he's suffering again without me?"

She resisted the urge to stroke Az's hair.

"All I want is him and all he wants is me. Is that hard to understand? Is it too much to ask that you let me be with him? Whatever else you want him to do, he'll do it. Just don't leave him like this. I can't stand it."

There was silence for a long moment.

"Why did you do this to me? Why did you choose me?" she asked. "My whole life I felt disconnected somehow. Adrift. Until him. He gave me a reason to live. A reason to be. We hated each other at first, but hate somehow turned to love. It's that love which allowed him to do what was necessary to save the world."

"I didn't choose you, Alice. I made you and I gave you to your parents to raise. They had no idea their daughter would house my punishment for my son. I created you to withstand its presence. You were born to be the vessel. Born to die at the hands of my son. It was the only way he'd truly learn who he is. The one to carry souls to their final resting place. He is death. It had to be at his hands."

A tear slid down her face. This was God's real plan.

"He needs me," she whispered. "Don't you see? I will help him carry out his duty. Help him stay the course. He belongs to me and I to him."

The entire time she'd been there, she'd not heard anything Az had said, but all at once, the sounds of his sobs echoed around the room.

"Take care of my son."

She turned, but he was gone. Looking down at Az again, she realised God had done as she asked. Given her back to him.

"Please, Father," Az whispered.

His head was still bowed. He didn't know she was there. She reached out, cupping his cheek with one hand. Az stiffened.

"Is this a trick? This feels like her, but I cannot believe it."

"Az, it is me," she said.

He raised his head to her slowly. Tears still welled in his eyes. Her heart pounded.

My angel. Still as perfect as the day we met. I love him like nothing else.

Silence permeated the air as they stared at each other.

He reached out, tugging her down to the floor. His mouth crashed down on hers. He pressed her down onto the marble floor, kissing her like he was drowning in her. His body covered hers. The familiar weight of him made her heart contract.

"Alice, my sweet Alice. You're alive. You're real. I love you so much. I didn't want the moment we said those words to each other to be our last, but now... now you're here."

"I love you," he whispered before he claimed her mouth again.

It was all she could do to let him take her under. She wanted to end his suffering at her death. There had always been something drawing them together. They needed each other. Even after he'd had to end her life, death couldn't keep them apart. He'd once told her she'd resent him when the time came, but she had never once felt that way. She'd understood. The Darkness couldn't be allowed to destroy the world.

He tugged her dress, pushing it up until it was pooled at her waist. He ripped off her underwear, his fingers sliding up her inner thighs. She arched up against him, desperately wanting to feel his touch yet hesitant because of where they were.

Really, Az? On the floor, right now? I love you, but I only just woke up. We should talk.

She didn't get a response. She couldn't deny his wild need made her feel wanted. His mouth against hers felt like home. He tugged at his own clothes, just enough to allow him to spring free. She cried out when he pushed inside her. She gripped his back. His pounding was merciless. Her whole body was on fire.

"I love you," she whispered. "I love you so much."

"Never leave me again. I cannot live without you, Alice. You are mine."

"Yours. Always."

The floor wasn't the most comfortable place to have an angel fuck your brains out, but she let it slide. He pinned one of her arms above her head, his lips fused to hers. This was where she belonged. With her angel. Nothing could separate them again.

It didn't take much for them both to cry out from a mutual conclusion. She panted beneath him, her heart pounding wildly in her chest. He peppered kisses across her chest and collarbone.

"You're real," he whispered.

"Mmm. I think we've established that now. You did just fuck me to make sure."

"Mmm, and I want to fuck you again."

He rested his forehead against hers.

"I wasn't sure if He would bring you back."

She wrapped her arms around his back, holding him to her.

"He and I had a conversation before He let you see me."

Az raised his head, staring down at her with wide eyes.

"Here, I'll show you," she continued, cupping his face.

She'd done this before when she'd shown him the visions she'd had of the Darkness. Only now, it was her conversation with God. It still felt so surreal. She'd had a conversation with the being who'd created everything.

"He asked you why you cared about me?" Az said.

"Clearly a human falling in love with an angel was weird for Him."

He shook his head, stroking her face.

"Mmm, it is not as if it hasn't happened before, but you and I are different. We belong together. Now and always." He frowned for a moment. "There's something different about you."

"Well I did die and come back to life."

"No. It's not that. You're still human and yet..."

He pulled away from her, sitting up. She felt bereft immediately.

"He's made you immortal."

"What? Why?"

It was her turn to sit up. How could she be immortal? She was human, wasn't she? It made no sense.

"Your conversation with Him. He said I would not continue in my duty without you. You haven't forgotten that I'm immortal. He's brought you back permanently. Forever. We really do have forever. Just like you wanted."

She looked down at her hands. There didn't seem to be anything different about her, yet she felt different on some level. The truth of what he'd said sunk in.

I'm immortal.

"Where are we?"

"In Heaven."

"He let you come home. He wants you to stay here, doesn't he? To fulfil your purpose."

"I imagine so."

Looking up at her angel, she felt a little dumbfounded. Did God expect her to remain here with Az, in Heaven?

"Does that mean I can't ever go back to Earth? What about my parents? I don't want them thinking I'm dead. Oh, but if He's made me immortal then I won't age. I won't be able to see them. Az, how is it even fair of Him to ask this of me? I know I asked Him to let me stay with you, but I didn't imagine it would be here, in Heaven."

He put cupped her face, brushing his thumb across her bottom lip. He gave her a soft smile, his green eyes glinting.

"Alice, we can see your parents. You forget, I'm an angel. As they age, I will make it appear though we are aging too. You don't need to worry about those things."

"You can do that?"

"You should know by now, I'd do anything for you. You are my world."

She edged closer to him, hating any sort of distance between them.

"Will He allow it?"

"With you by my side, I will do as He asks. He doesn't have a say in what we do outside of that time. He knows I am yours to command. Always, my sweet Alice, always."

Her heart was in her mouth. The Az before her was different to the one she'd met all those weeks ago on that park bench. He was open and free with his affection. He didn't suffer in the same way. He had saved the world from destruction and now he was home.

Could she really make this place her home too? Could Heaven be where she lived out the rest of their lives by each other's sides? Was there really any question of what she wanted to do?

No. There's no question. I love him. Azrael is mine. I am his. That's all that matters. The rest is inconsequential.

"I love you, Az. I'll be wherever you are. Forever. All I want is you."

The way his eyes shone at her words made her heart sing. He reached for her, picking her up off the floor. He walked her towards the doors she'd come through and back into the bedroom. He set her down before tugging her dress off. He discarded his own clothes at the foot of the bed. They lay in the soft sheets together. Az clutched Alice to his chest. She felt the hammering of his heart against her fingertips. This was where she was meant to be.

"My heart is yours," he whispered, kissing the top of her head.

"And mine belongs to you," she replied, smiling.

Heaven was her new home.

And Azrael the Archangel of Death was her everything.

Epilogue

Alice sat at the edge of the pool, feet dangling over the side. It had been a few weeks since she'd returned to Earth to visit her parents. They were none the wiser that their daughter now resided in Heaven. It didn't always feel right lying to them, but she was grateful she was able to maintain a relationship with them. One day they would be gone and she would still be here, frozen in time.

It no longer bothered her that she was now immortal. It had been strange at first, but as the months ticked by, she found it was nothing to be afraid of. Not when she had her angel by her side. She smiled. Azrael would be back soon. She had been given her own set of duties in Heaven, but it was never anything taxing. She helped some of the Guardian Angels watch over their charges.

She stared down the reflection pool. She liked to keep track of what was happening down on Earth to the people she'd met. The ones who had helped Az against the Darkness. All of them seemed to be doing well.

Izzy and Rex's baby girl was now six months old. Little Luna had beautiful green, gold eyes like her father and blonde hair like her mother. They'd got married not long after she'd been born, in a simple civil ceremony. Alice and Azrael had managed to attend at the last minute. The party afterwards had gone on late into the night. A huge bonfire had been erected in the back garden of Alistair's house. Many of the werewolves and other shifters had changed into their animal forms. It really was a sight to behold.

Grace and Alistair were running their own business together. He'd opened up a little shop in Camden, selling potions and herbs to the supernatural community. He still kept clients on the side. Izzy had told Alice that the two of them were talking about getting married, although Grace kept insisting it was too soon. Alistair and Izzy had become best friends. He and Grace were godparents to little Luna.

Alice had forgiven Gavin, for trying to kill her. She felt like she owed it to him after the Darkness had killed his wife and forced her to become one of the undead. Daisy seemed to be adjusting to life as a vampire slowly. Despite Neave's reluctance to become a sire, there were no issues between any of them. Alice could only be glad. She liked the fiery, dark-haired girl. She'd become more involved in helping Gavin run his territory and had been accepted by the Vampire Council.

The two people Alice had become closest to were Lukas and Ella. Both of them had visited Heaven often to see Ella's mother, Ariel and Lukas' father, the Archangel Michael. Now the Darkness was gone, they were still working for Hell, but now they also worked for Heaven. She was glad the two of them had found a new purpose.

She smiled. Seeing all of her supernatural friends made her long to return to the world of humanity. She was no longer a part of that world though. Heaven was her home. Heaven is where she belonged.

A pair of arms encircled her waist.

"Mmm, I have missed you," he whispered, peppering kisses down the back of her neck.

"We saw each other mere hours ago," she replied.

"And yet it is never enough."

She turned, looking up at her beautiful angel.

"Someone is very impatient."

"How can I not be? Knowing you're here, waiting for me, it's all I can do to stop myself rushing home to you."

Soft lips met hers in a tender kiss. It sent tingles up her spine. His touch always did.

"My angel," she whispered, pulling away.

"Come, I have a surprise for you."

He helped her to her feet after she swung her legs back.

"A surprise?"

He took her hand, leading her towards the door.

"Mmm."

She cocked an eyebrow, but didn't ask any further questions. He wouldn't tell her even if she begged. There was more than enough begging when they were alone and he was driving her wild with his words, his touch. She shook herself. There would always be time for that later.

When they reached Heaven's Gates, Alice turned to him with confusion.

"Why are we returning to Earth?"

"You'll see."

It was dark by the time they landed in a very familiar setting. The street lamps in Hyde Park twinkled. Az smiled at her, his green eyes glinting. She felt his power wash over her and looked down. She was wearing a beautiful white, flowing dress with twinkling stars embroidered into the skirt. When she looked up, he was in a blue, three piece suit.

"Azrael, what on earth is this about?" she asked.

"Patience."

He took her hand, leading her through the trees into a clearing. Someone had strung up fairy lights in the trees and around an archway set near them. She put a hand on her mouth. Gathered there were not only her parents, but all of her supernatural friends and lastly, her best friend, Chris. Tears welled in her eyes.

"Az... What is this?" she whispered.

"Whilst it may not be legally binding as we do not technically exist in the mortal world, you father has always wanted to see his little girl get married."

"Married? You mean... this is our wedding?"

"Yes, my heart."

"I can't believe you did this without telling me."

"Mmm, but you wouldn't have agreed otherwise."

She shoved him. He was right. All of it seemed ridiculous because they were bound to each other. He'd done this for her parents. He grinned at her, taking her hand.

"Shall we?" he asked.

She nodded, unable to say any more words. He led her towards the archway, her friends grinning at them from ear to ear. Her mum and dad looked so proud and Chris gave her a wink and a thumbs up.

Standing in the archway was Michael.

"You were in on this too?" she asked.

Azrael had made up with his fellow Archangels. She could only be glad he had his family back again.

"Of course. Are you ready?" Michael replied.

She looked up at Azrael. She was more than ready to become his wife even if it was just for show. Alice loved him with every inch of her being. He smiled back at her, radiant as always. He glowed softly, his halo appearing above his head. He had always been beautiful to her. And he was hers forever.

"Yes. Let's do this."

Lucifer lay on his bed, his arms folded behind his head. It was typical. Azrael was allowed to return home and yet he was still stuck down here in Hell. He knew he was fulfilling his purpose as the Devil. It did not prevent him from resenting the fact. This wasn't what he wanted. He had always needed to be free. As an angel, he was caged by his father's needs and expectations.

He turned over on his side, feeling anger coursing through his veins. Why had his brother been granted a reprieve? Why had their father even gone so far as to send his wrath to end everything only for it to be a ruse to teach Azrael a lesson? And his damn brother was living it up in Heaven with his human girl. The girl he'd killed and God had brought back and granted immortality to.

He'd seen Azrael when he'd returned to Earth with her in tow. It irritated him no end, yet he wasn't mad at his brother. No. He was angry with their father. He was the cause of all of this. Of forcing his son to punish those who had lived terrible lives. They might deserve it, yet he resented his duty. He would never be free of this burden. This curse.

Even so, he found himself revelling in his position. He ruled Hell. He was the king. But one day, he would make sure his father regretted his actions. One day, God would come to understand that he couldn't keep angels under his thumb any longer. They deserved freedom as much as humanity did. Lucifer would see to it that God learnt his lesson.

He sat up as a purple light appeared in the ceiling.

What the fuck is that?

Acknowledgements

Thank you for reading this book. As an indie author, reviews are very important to me. I hope you consider leaving one if you enjoyed it.

This book has been an epic journey for me. Book five was going to end the overreaching story arc I'd started in Demon's Destiny. In that sense, it had a lot to live up to. A lot of questions needed answering. I wanted a unique ending for my characters and to tie up the loose ends.

Whilst I was writing Cursed Heart, the concept for Death's Angel popped up in my head. This damn angel would not get out of my head. He was demanding, insistent and I only had one question.

'What is your name?'

I did a little research and the name Azrael came up. Perfect, I thought. Then I checked and found that he was known as the angel of death. And from there, the story unfolded before my eyes. Here I was trying to get Cursed Heart written and Azrael demanded my attention unlike any other character I've had before. I had to give in. I ended up writing about one fourth of the book because he wouldn't let up until I got him down on the page.

Whilst I did go back and finish up Cursed Heart, Azrael still played on my mind. Him and Alice were these two people who were so lost in the world. They needed each other in a way I hadn't even imagined.

I'll readily admit, when I wrote Demon's Destiny, I had absolutely no idea how I was going to bring the Darkness to life. So, it came as a surprise to me when I discovered that Alice was going to be its vessel. And not only that, but Azrael was destined to kill her. This whole book took me on an unexpected journey, from the introduction of Lucifer, Alice and Azrael's love for each other and ultimately, writing God. I knew at some point he would have to arrive on the scene. He is such an important aspect of Azrael and

Lucifer's exile. It was incredibly daunting to write him, but the God in this world is complex and his motivations are never clear. I enjoyed that sense of ambiguity.

Bringing these characters to life has been an absolute joy. Especially since I was able to bring all five of my couples into this book. Getting them all together on the page was terrifying and difficult, but it was always my intention for this to be the last book. I wanted to tie up their storylines in a fitting way and I really hope I achieved that.

(As you know, there is another book and I cannot wait to share Lucifer's story with you all too!)

Death's Angel really has been a labour of love and I'm so, so happy it's finally in the world.

There are a few very important people I wish to thank for being there when I was writing this book.

I'd like to give a huge shout out to Thunder Team Alpha Force. Sean, Katie, Gil, Paul, Kenny, Corry, Jordan and Marnye, you guys are incredible. My Twitter Gang! I met them not long after I released Demon's Destiny and they have been there for me through the ups and downs of this publishing journey. I couldn't do without them. They make me laugh every single day. And their support has got me through some dark times.

I know I dedicated this book to her, but I again must thank the ever wonderful, Sabrina. She has been the greatest friend I could've ever hoped for. She was with me every step of the way when I wrote this book. She knew all about the trials I went through dealing with the demanding angel and even gave me inspiration. All I can say is... cloud sex. She'll know what that means! I love you, Sab!

Big thank you to my mum for reading Death's Angel before anyone else. Her description of Azrael and Alice's relationship will stay with me forever.

'A tale of two lost introverts. Doing extraordinary things.'

And last, but not least, I will always thank my ever wonderful and supportive husband, Steve. Without him, I wouldn't be on this journey. My heart is yours forever.

About the Author

Born and raised in Sussex, UK near the Ashdown Forest where she grew up climbing trees and building Lego towns with her younger brother. Sarah fell in love with novels when she was a teenager reading her aunt's historical regency romances. She's always had a love of the supernatural, avidly devouring paranormal romances and TV shows such as True Blood and Supernatural.

Sarah currently resides in Berkshire with her husband. Music is one of her biggest inspirations and she always has something on in the background whilst writing. She is an avid gamer and is often found hogging her husband's Xbox.

Sign up to her mailing list to find out about her latest releases, promotions and giveaways below:
www.subscribepage.com/sarahbaileywriter

You can find more about Sarah Bailey in the following ways:
www.sarahbaileywriter.com
www.facebook.com/sbaileyauthor
www.twitter.com/sbaileyauthor
www.instagram.com/sbaileyauthor

The Sequel to Death's Angel

Lucifer's Cage

Hell is closed for business. And the Devil is about to meet his match.

The King of Hell is having a bad year. The gates to his kingdom are sealed. His demons are restless. And when Candace, a half fae girl, drops out of a portal on top of him, she complicates things further. Not only is she not supposed to be in Hell, she proves to be feisty, fearless and undeniably tempting.

Candace is furious at Jax, her best friend, for landing her in Hell. Lucifer, the original fallen angel, has a way of driving her crazy. And the biggest problem of all? He wants her and her secrets. Ones she must keep at all costs.

With only a few months left till her birthday and her family duty looming over her head, she has to find a way to go home. And she most definitely cannot fall in deep with the Devil.

Will they find a way to reopen the Gates of Hell? And will Lucifer discover who Candace really is before it's too late?

If you want to hear more about this new release and others, please sign up to Sarah's mailing list:
www.subscribepage.com/sarahbaileywriter

Made in the USA
San Bernardino, CA
22 December 2018